MARSHFIELD 1919

The Story of Wayne Schooley

MARK GENGLER

by Mark Gengler

NOAH THORNE
A WISCONSIN FARM BOY IN THE 1920'S

THANKS A LOT GOD

WOLF CREEK CIDER
THE STORY OF AARON STROUD

MIGRANT!
THE STORY OF DANNY BROOME

MARSHFIELD 1919
THE STORY OF WAYNE SCHOOLEY

DEDICATION

This novel is dedicated to all the men and women of the armed forces, past, present and future. Yours is the truest form of patriotism. You willingly defend your country, giving your life, if necessary, to pass on a free America to generations of all races and religions. Thank you.

MARSHFIELD 1919

The Story of Wayne Schooley

MARK GENGLER

SOUL FIRE PRESS

MARSHFIELD 1919 *The Story of Wayne Schooley*
by Mark Gengler

Published by

SOUL FIRE PRESS, *an imprint of Christopher Matthews Publishing*
PO Box 571
Gleneden Beach, OR 97388

Interior layout, cover design by Suzanne Parrott
Cover art: *Landscape with Cattle*. Artist Jan Kobell (II), 1804, rijksmuseum.nl

Genre: *Juvenile, Young Adult, prohibition, clean read, historical, bootleggers, farming, harvesting, romance, friendship, WWI, Spanish flu*

ISBN: 978-1-944072-73-5 (pb)

10 9 8 7 6 5 4 3 2 1

Printed in the
United States of America

CHAPTER ONE

The nurse held a cool cloth to his forehead as he labored to draw each breath. The coarse sheets were damp from his sweat. Only 21 years old, Sergeant Wayne Schooley lay limp on his hospital bed at Fort Meade, Maryland, as the flu virus filled his lungs. His fever of 102 degrees had held steady for two days as he drew each ragged breath. His strong five-foot-11 inch body slowly wasted away as he fought to stay alive.

Wayne had arrived back in America four days earlier, on March 10th, 1919, aboard the troop ship USS *Cutler*. The war was over, and the men were coming home. A great shout had arisen as the Statue of Liberty was sighted. Later, as the soldiers disembarked, a few had been coughing, and some felt dizzy. Then, on the train to Fort Meade to sign his discharge papers, the fever came upon Wayne and several other men. Arriving at the Fort, Doctors waited to check the soldiers for signs of the dreaded flu virus spreading rapidly across the country. Two dozen men, Wayne among them, had been admitted to the hospital.

Doctors had no known cure for the virus—only aspirin, to lessen the pain and fever, and fluids whenever possible. By day seven, Wayne seemed to be recovering. His temperature was down to 100 degrees and his breathing, though still rough, was steady. The nurses spoon-fed him chicken broth. On the evening of day eight, the fever spiked to 104, lasted until dawn, and then broke. By noon Wayne's temperature had dropped to 99, and his breathing was almost normal. He drank water and ate a bowl of soup.

"How long have I been here?" he asked the nurse.

Slipping the thermometer under his tongue, she replied, "You arrived nine days ago with twenty-three other men."

"How are the others doing?"

As she took his pulse, the nurse slowly shook her head. "Only you survived. I never saw a person fight so hard to live."

On the morning of March 24th, the hospital released Wayne Schooley. He reported to the Headquarters building to sign his discharge papers and receive mustering out pay. Instead, a Captain handed him an envelope and said, "The Army owes you $125. We thank you for your time in uniform."

Wayne caught a ride to the train station and bought a one-way ticket to Marshfield, Wisconsin, his hometown. As the train rolled westward, he read the newspaper purchased at the station. Europe was in ruins. The constant shelling in France and Germany had wiped out entire villages. Thousands of starving people resorted to eating horsemeat just to stay alive. And as they traveled, the virus spread from place to place, killing nearly all it touched.

America was not faring any better. Large cities like New York, Boston, and Chicago were hardest hit, with hundreds of deaths reported daily. The sickness also ravaged small towns, killing young and old alike. Most died within 48 hours, some lingered for days before passing, and very few recovered. The last letter Wayne received from home was dated October 1918 by his father, Erwin. "Your mother Julia has a bad cold. She may need to be hospitalized." Wayne had not received the letter until January 1919, as his unit had been constantly on the move, driving back the German Army until the truce was signed on November 11th, 1918.

Erwin Schooley worked as an accountant at the Farmers & Merchants Bank in Marshfield. His wife, Julia, was on the school board and active in the Lutheran church. Wayne was their only child. Erwin loved the outdoors—fishing in the summer, hunting in the fall and winter—and shared this with his son.

On Wayne's tenth birthday, he got his first firearm, a double-barreled Fox .410 shotgun. On his 12th birthday, he received his first rifle, a Winchester Model 94 in .32 special caliber. Father and son spent many happy days enjoying the bounty that Wisconsin had to offer.

Julia loved to knit. Caps, scarves, gloves, and colorful afghans flowed from her hands. Baking also was a passion, especially pies. Her strawberry-rhubarb and Dutch apple pies were always in demand at church socials.

Wayne worked as a teller at his father's bank when President Woodrow Wilson announced America's entry into the great war in April 1917. Many of the local young men rushed to join the Military. However, Wayne waited and had many heated discussions with his parents about enlisting. Finally, in July, Wayne joined the U.S. Army and reported for training at Fort Knox, Kentucky.

The troop ship USS *Georgia* arrived in France in early November, carrying Private Wayne Schooley and thousands of other young men. Also on board were tons of supplies to be unloaded—tents, crates of canned food, blankets, medical supplies, artillery shells—all necessary articles to supply an Army going to war.

A young Captain named Higgins from the Quartermaster Corps was responsible for the men unloading the ship. He paid particular attention to Private Schooley, who seemed to be a natural leader. He passed the word to his commander, and soon Wayne was assigned to the Captains Company and promoted to Corporal. However, the trenches on the western front would not lay claim to this young man.

CHAPTER TWO

The conductor gently shook Wayne's shoulder. "Your ticket, please, sir," he said softly.

Reaching in his uniform, Wayne handed his ticket to the older man. "I must have dozed off," Wayne said with a yawn. "Where are we?"

"We just crossed into Indiana and will be making a two-hour stop soon in Greendale," the conductor told him. "If you're hungry, there is a cafe in the station."

The sun was setting as the train left Greendale. Coffee, a ham and cheese sandwich, and apple pie had sated his appetite. The coach car was about half full of people headed north and west. Wayne's thoughts returned to France and his role in the war to end all wars.

He remembered the horses and wagons first used to deliver needed supplies to the front lines. The teamsters were almost all French. Some spoke and understood English, though many did not. In the end, it didn't make any difference. All the drivers knew where they were going and how to get there.

"We need more blankets and coffee," yelled a Doctor from the Medical tent. "Next time, bring some tobacco for my pipe," a Major said. Wayne wrote down what the men wanted and hoped he could deliver.

On return trips, wounded soldiers would ride back to the hospital. There were ambulances, but they were almost always full to overflowing. After each delivery, the wagons were cleaned and made ready for the next trip.

"This is no way to fight a war!" General John J. "Black Jack" Pershing met with the French and British Generals at headquarters. "To defeat your enemy, you must attack and drive him back. You cannot win fighting from a hole in the ground!" The British Army agreed. In fact, they had been busy designing and building the first tanks. The French were also working on a tank, and after trials and errors in battle, The French Mark IV built by Renault proved to be the winner. A newly promoted Lt. Colonel, George S. Patton, was chosen by General Pershing to organize the first Tank Brigade.

Sergeant Wayne Schooley was dockside when the Ford trucks and ambulances rolled off the supply ship. "We need to find men who can drive a truck," Wayne told Captain Higgins.

"I've got 24 men ready, and if we need more, I'll get them," said Higgins. As long as the gasoline supplies were delivered, the days of horses and mules in the U.S. Army would soon end. A line of vehicles moved slowly from the wharf to warehouses, where they would load supplies for the front lines. It was August of 1918, and the roads were dusty and uneven. Soon the fall rains would come bringing the cold, sticky mud. Wayne remembered the mud and how they used horses to move the stuck and mired trucks.

The rocking motion of the train lulled Wayne into sleep again. He awoke hours later as the Conductor entered the coach car. "Next stop is Chicago. There is a two hour layover, then on to Milwaukee."

It was after midnight, but the diner in the station was busy. "A bowl of chicken soup, a cheese sandwich and coffee," Wayne said to the tired-looking waitress. As he sipped the hot coffee, Wayne noticed other uniforms in the crowd. A half-dozen Navy, three Marines, and one other Army—a Major limping slowly with a cane, on his way out the door. The waitress arrived with his food, and Wayne realized he was hungry for the first time in days.

Back in the coach car, Wayne spotted the Major sitting by a window. "May I join you sir?" he asked.

With a tired smile, the Major held out his hand. "Major Charles Stieber. Please have a seat." Settling in, Wayne inquired about the man's leg. Leaning forward on his cane, the Major said it was "broken by a German bullet in the Muse-Argonne. My war ended there. Tell me about you, Sergeant."

Wayne explained his role in the Quartermaster Corps and his bout with the Spanish Flu.

"You are one of the very few to survive the lung fever," said the Major.

As the miles rolled on, they talked of the constant artillery fire, the tanks, and the Armistice. "The Germans simply ran out of everything," the Major said softly.

"A Colonel told me later his Brigade captured a German platoon boiling harness leather for soup. They had already eaten the horse." Wayne talked about the groups of German soldiers who had just walked into British field Headquarters and surrendered. "They all carried rifles, but none had any ammunition, not a single bullet."

In Milwaukee, they parted, the Major going north to Green Bay. The gray shadows of dawn showed on the horizon as Wayne changed trains for Marshfield. As he stepped into the coach car, he saw every seat was full. The Conductor came forward and motioned Wayne to follow him. Taking Wayne through the club car, he led him into first class. Sinking softly into the plush cushion, he closed his eyes and smiled. When he opened them again, a porter was standing there. "Would the gentleman like a drink?" he asked.

"A hot coffee with a half-shot of brandy would be fine," said Wayne.

The rising sun showed patches of snow and dirty snowbanks left by the snowplows. A few stalks of corn missed by the pickers dotted the unplowed fields. Cows stood leisurely eating from outside hay racks as a milk truck waited at a crossing. The driver waved as the train passed. It was good to be going home.

CHAPTER THREE

Wayne watched from the window as the train eased into the station. The town looked the same—the businesses, streets, and people—but there were differences too. More automobiles crowded the road, even a motorcycle. A Packard touring car waited for some lucky passenger. A Studebaker truck with the tailgate down, waiting for freight. Shouldering his duffel bag, Wayne stepped down to the platform.

An older man approached, tipped his hat, and said, "My name is Tom. Would you like a taxi, sir?"

Wayne nodded. "Take me to 114 Benson Ave." It was his parents' home, where he had grown up.

A feeling of dread crept over Wayne as he stepped from the Taxi. The front lawn was overgrown with weeds poking through the snow. The house windows were dirty and old newspapers littered the front porch. He tried the front door, which was locked. Walking around the side of the house, Wayne noticed the carriage shed door was open. Inside sat his father's Model T Ford with one rear tire flat. A silent tremor coursed through him as he stood there. Tears misted his eyes as his head slowly sank to his chest. His parents were dead. The flu had claimed two more. He felt a hand on his back and turned his head to look. The taxi driver had waited, knowing this was not the homecoming his passenger had expected.

"Can I take you somewhere?" he asked.

Thinking a moment, Wayne nodded. "The bank. I need to go to the bank and find out what happened."

The bank manager, Arnold Gehrke, ushered Wayne into his office. "Erwin and Julia died in October," he said. "The flu claimed both of them. We tried to notify you but were unable to reach you."

"I imagine they were laid to rest by the church," Wayne said.

"Reverend Wilkey took care of everything. Sadly, he lost half of his congregation to the flu." Arnold then opened a desk drawer and took out a manila envelope. "The passing of your parents has left me the unfortunate duty of administering their estate." Arnold withdrew several papers and spread them out on the desk. "Your parents owned the house, and it is yours to do with as you wish. Erwin left a savings account balance of four thousand dollars and a Life Insurance benefit of five thousand dollars. These are now yours." He handed Wayne a passbook saying, "The total funds are on account here and will be transferred to your name."

Wayne signed several papers, and Arnold handed him the keys to the house. "Reverend Wilkey has not yet ordered a gravestone. I am sure he would like your advice as to the inscriptions." He rose slowly and held out his hand. "If I may be of any further assistance. Please call me."

Walking slowly through the cemetery, Reverend Wilkey took Wayne to his parents' gravesite. "Your father chose the plots several years ago. Their caskets were donated by the church board, of which your mother was a member." Pausing a moment, he laid his hand on Wayne's arm. "Why God called them home and mercifully spared you is beyond our simple understanding. We must trust there was a reason if we are to move forward." The two men stood in silent prayer, bidding farewell to the departed.

Later that evening, Wayne walked through an empty house where memories waited in every room. The pictures on the walls, the Edison phonograph his father had been so proud of, his mother's chair with the ball of yarn laying on the seat, and his father's hat, still resting on the small table in the entryway.

Pictures of deer and ducks still hung on the walls in his bedroom, each chosen with great care years ago. His clothing in the dresser was all clean and folded; his suit, some dress shirts, and a jacket hung in the closet with shoes and boots lined up neatly beneath. On the far wall, the gun rack his father had helped him build held his shotgun and rifle. Sitting on the bed, Wayne decided he would donate as much of his parents' belongings as possible to the church. Sinking back on the bed, the events of the day washed over him. Then, finally, he drifted into a deep, dreamless sleep.

The barking of someone's dog woke him just before dawn. He rose slowly, feeling rested but weak. A hot bath and shave revived him enough to realize he was hungry. Wayne hung his uniform in the closet and dressed in jeans and a blue plaid shirt and boots. There was no food in the house, not even coffee. I need to do some shopping, he thought. He stepped outside, heading toward the carriage shed. The Ford would need to be checked over before driving. A gust of wind showered him with snowflakes, a reminder that winter in Wisconsin was being its usual unpredictable self.

Back in the house, Wayne descended the basement stairs. The furnace was a coal-fed monster that needed food. Soon the heat rose through the vents, taking the chill from the air. After washing up in the kitchen, Wayne sat at the table and made a list of what needed to be done. Stuffing the list in his shirt pocket, he put on his winter coat from the hall closet. Then, almost as an afterthought, he picked up his father's hat from the entry table and put it on. With a smile, he realized it fit.

Carson's Cafe was about half-full when he entered. The brisk four-block walk had given him an appetite. Taking a seat at the counter, Wayne looked around but saw no familiar faces. Finally, the older waitress, whose name tag read Millie, pulled a pencil from behind her ear and asked, "What can I getcha?"

"Coffee, pancakes, and bacon," said Wayne.

Millie laid the check in front of Wayne as he finished his coffee. Then, on a hunch, he asked her, "Who would I talk to about hiring a good housekeeper?"

With a big smile, Millie answered, "You talk to me! My sister Janice is looking for work. She can cook, clean, and do laundry."

Writing his name and address on a scrap of paper, he handed it to Millie, saying, "I don't have the telephone hooked up yet. Ask her if she will come by the house this afternoon."

BANG! BANG! Everyone in the Cafe jumped up and looked around. The front door flew open, and a boy stuck his head in, yelling, "They're robbing the Savings & Loan!"

Across the street was the Marshfield Savings & Loan. Wayne watched a man back out of the door, a pistol in one hand and a bag in the other, followed by a second man with a gun. Then, suddenly, a Dodge screeched to a stop in the middle of the road, and a tall man in uniform wearing a gun belt got out holding a shotgun.

"Drop the guns and lay on the ground," he yelled. The man holding the bag raised his pistol, aiming it at the man in the hat. BANG! The shotgun blast picked the robber right off his feet, and he fell backward on the sidewalk. The other robber tossed down his pistol and lay on the ground.

"That's sheriff Billy Anderson," Millie said.

CHAPTER FOUR

Wayne knew Sheriff William T. 'Billy' Anderson. He was one of his father's oldest friends, and they had hunted and fished together since grade school. Billy's daughter Cassie was a year younger than Wayne, and he had taken her to his Senior Prom in High School. Wayne stepped out onto the sidewalk as the Sheriff approached, holding out his hand. "Glad to see you made it home, son," the Sheriff said. "I'm a little busy just now, but you stop and see me when you get settled in."

Wayne spent the rest of the morning getting the telephone service in use, having the Model T towed in and gone over, ordering ice for the icebox in the kitchen, and stopping by the market for eggs, bread, milk, and coffee. As he neared his house, he saw a bicycle with a large wire basket on the front and one on the back leaning against the porch railing. A stout middle-aged woman dressed in men's clothing sat on the porch step, smoking a hand-rolled cigarette.

"You must be Janice," Wayne said with a smile. Tossing the cigarette aside, she stood, stepped down from the porch, and held out her hand.

"I'm Janice Magnuson. Call me Jan. Millie told me that you needed a housekeeper. I can start today if you want. I charge $15 a week, and I don't smoke in the house."

Jan helped Wayne to fill two large boxes with his parents' clothes. First, he set aside a few things of his father's. Then, out of curiosity, he asked, "why do you wear men's clothes?"

"If you ever had a cold wind blow up your butt on a cold day you wouldn't need to ask," Jan answered with a grin.

Smiling back, he said, "If you find something you like please take it."

Jan pointed to a small pile of clothes by the door. "I figured you wouldn't mind, so I did, thanks."

As they closed up the boxes, the telephone rang. Answering it, Wayne was informed he now had telephone service. Then, a honking horn made him glance out the kitchen window. Tyler 'Snuffy' Bigelow was backing his tow truck up to the garage. Putting on his coat as he walked out the back door, Wayne warmly greeted an old friend.

Spitting out the pinch of snuff from his jaw, Snuffy was grinning from ear to ear. "Sure is good to see you pal, glad you made it home. Sorry about your folks."

"I'm happy you got back alive too," Wayne said. "I heard the Army kept you busy fixing their trucks in France."

"They sure did. Dad ran the garage while I was gone so we stayed in business. I'll have this Model T back in a day or two, good as new!"

"I would make you a supper, but you got no food in the house," Jan yelled from the kitchen. Wayne handed her a twenty-dollar bill. "Get as much as your bicycle can carry. A stew would hit the spot."

"I'll be back in an hour and make you the best beef stew you ever had."

Wayne finished sorting through his father's papers and

found two bills that needed to be paid. Tied with a blue ribbon were the letters he had written during basic training and from France. In a cardboard folder was the wedding picture of Erwin and Julia, taken at the studio here in town. These things would be saved in a box and stored on his closet shelf.

Jan had returned from the market with both baskets full and a box balanced on the handlebars. "I spent the whole twenty dollars plus two of my own which you can add to my pay," Jan said as she began unloading the bicycle. "Help me get all this food in the house, then get me some wood for the stove. Today I'll cook, tomorrow I'll start cleaning."

After a delicious supper of stew, Jan chased him from the house. "I'll clean up here, and I'll be back tomorrow morning at seven sharp," she warned. The air was cold, but the snow flurries had stopped. Wayne remembered walking to the grade school with Cassie and several other friends. Sheriff Billy Anderson lived one block up from Wayne. The porch light was on when he knocked on the front door. It opened, and a plump, smiling lady named Helen, Billy's wife, greeted him with a hug.

"Let me look at you," Helen declared. "You come right into the kitchen. Billy and I are having coffee. Let me get you a cup." It was like being home with a different set of parents. Wayne's mother Julia had always said, 'Cassie is the daughter we never had, and you are the son the Anderson's never had.'

Billy pulled out a chair, and Helen set down the coffee. "Are you getting the house in shape?" Billy asked.

"I hired a housekeeper, Jan Magnuson," Wayne told them. Both Billy and Helen broke out laughing.

"You have got a real character on your hands now," Billy said. "Don't get me wrong, she's the best in town, but she does things her way and to hell with what people think."

Raising his cup, Wayne said, "In that case we should get along fine."

Helen chased the men into the living room while she cleaned the kitchen. Billy eased into his favorite overstuffed chair while Wayne sat on the sofa.

"Have you made any plans on what you will do for a job?" Billy asked slowly.

"I hadn't really thought about it yet," Wayne answered.

Leaning forward, elbows on his knees, Billy said, "In January, all the states ratified the new prohibition bill. When it gets voted into law, and I'm sure it will, I'm going to have to hire at least two more deputies. All I have now is Vernon Fromme, and he is only part-time and fifty-years-old. I need younger men, like you, that I can depend on."

Caught off guard, Wayne was quiet for a few moments. "I need a little time to think it over Billy. Can I let you know in a few days?"

Billy nodded, and they shook hands.

CHAPTER FIVE

"Any news from Cassie, how is she?" Wayne asked.

"Cassie graduates from nursing school in Minneapolis the first of May," Helen said with a sigh. "It's wonderful but also sad."

"Cassie was engaged to a doctor who joined the Army about the same time you did," Billy said. "A fine young man who we met only once."

A small tear escaped Helen's eye. Then, dabbing at it with her handkerchief, she explained. "His name was David Blake. He was working at a field Hospital in France when an artillery shell hit the tent he was working in."

"She's coming home to work at St. Joseph's hospital here in Marshfield," Billy said. "She'll be really glad to see you."

Walking home, Wayne thought about Cassie, his friend from childhood. They had shared secrets, told each other their dreams, argued, cried, and laughed together through their teen years. Unfortunately, they had drifted apart when Cassie decided to attend nursing school. It would be great to see her again.

Wayne was up, dressed, and making coffee the following morning when Jan knocked on the door at seven sharp.

"I need a house key, in case you're gone," she told Wayne as she walked in. "Now let's have coffee and then you go downtown for breakfast while I get to work."

The aroma of hot food and coffee filled the air as Wayne entered Carson's Cafe. He got an empty table for two in the corner just as Millie set down his coffee.

"Jan must have kicked you out while she was cleaning," Millie said with a grin.

Laughing, Wayne told her, "I don't plan on going back till late this afternoon. How about some eggs, hash-browns, and bacon this morning?"

Millie wrote it down and moved to the next table.

"I heard you were back in town," said a familiar voice. It belonged to Wayne's old friend Lyle Peterson, who pulled out a chair and sat. At 5 foot 10 inches tall, Lyle was built square but lean. The two shook hands while Millie set down his coffee and took Lyle's order.

"Sorry to hear about your folks, lost Mom to the damn flu," Lyle said sadly.

"What's keeping you busy these days?" Wayne asked.

"Working part time at the sawmill stacking lumber. Otherwise, looking for a better job."

"I think I might be able to find one for you," Wayne said.

Wayne told Lyle about Billy Anderson needing deputies. "I thought about it last night and this morning, and I think it might be interesting work."

"Anything would be better than the sawmill. I'd like to know what it pays and how much training we'd need."

"I will call Billy tonight and find out. Do you have an auto?" Wayne asked.

"Don't have an auto, just an Indian motorcycle," Lyle told him, "it has a sidecar and will do seventy-five on the highway." Millie set down their food, and they ate.

Wayne's next stop was the garage.

"I got it running, but you might have a burnt valve. It's smoking a little," Snuffy told him.

"It's a 1913." Wayne sighed. "I should probably trade it in for a new one."

Snuffy pointed down the street. "I know just the car for you. The Ford dealer, Harry Mason, just took in a 1918 Studebaker. I checked it over for him, and it's in great shape."

Wayne nodded his head. "How much do I owe you?"

Snuffy waved him off. "All I did was patch the inner tube, no charge."

The Studebaker was a black sedan with whitewall tires. Chewing on a cigar, Harry Mason said, "I can let you have this fine auto for $300 and your Model T. It's a one owner with only 375 miles on it. Runs like new."

"Get it ready to go," Wayne told him, "I'll go to the bank and get you a check."

"No offense," Harry said, "but I prefer cash."

Snuffy was right; the Studebaker was a smooth-running auto. Wayne drove to the Lutheran church to talk to Reverend Wilkey.

"We will gladly accept any donations you have," said the Reverend, "there are always families in need of assistance."

"I will bring them here this afternoon," Wayne said.

Jan helped him load the two boxes into the Studebaker.

"I warmed up some stew for lunch," Jan said, "but tonight you get pork chops and baked potatoes."

"I want you to have supper with me," Wayne told her, "I hate eating alone."

Jan's round face broke into a big smile. "I've never turned down a free meal and, it just so happens that pork chops are one of my favorites."

After Jan left, Wayne called Billy Anderson and told him about Lyle Peterson.

"I know Lyle. I think he would make a good Deputy," said Billy. "Why don't you both stop by my office tomorrow morning and we can go over all the details."

Later, walking through the house Wayne marveled at the fine job Jan was doing. Stepping onto the back porch, he looked over the old hand crank washing machine. *Need a new machine*, he thought. *One with a gasoline-powered motor.* He'd ask Jan tomorrow.

The following day Jan had a better idea. "You've got a big kitchen with electricity," she said. "Benbow's Appliance store has an electric powered Maytag washer, and they deliver." Then, pointing to the corner with the broom closet, she said, "you can store it in there. It's on wheels, so I can move it anywhere I want."

Nodding his head, Wayne agreed. "I'll call them today and have them bring one over." Jan was all smiles. "I like working for you. You're not afraid of progress. That earns you a peach pie tonight."

"What do I do with the old machine?" Wayne asked.

"Moses Rickert will pick it up for junk," Jan said.

CHAPTER SIX

The Sheriff's office was added to the Marshfield Police Dept. building ten years ago. It wasn't much: a 20 x 20-foot square room with a stove, two file cabinets, two chairs, a gun rack on one wall, a map of the county took up another wall and a wood desk with a rolling chair. Billy sat behind the desk and handed some paperwork to Wayne and Lyle seated in front of him.

"You men are just what I have been hoping to find," said Billy. "You're young, in good shape, and able to take orders. Sign these papers, and let's get down to business." After signing and handing the papers back, Billy continued.

"Your pay is $225 a month. You will take a two-week training course at Camp McCoy starting Monday next week. You will stay at the camp in the old barracks and eat in the mess hall."

"What about transportation?" asked Lyle.

"You use your own vehicles and get reimbursed for the gas," Billy said.

"Do we get a sidearm?" Wayne asked.

"I purchased six .38 special Colt revolvers from the Army after the war," Billy said with a smile, "and they all work just fine. You can take your pick."

Over lunch at Carson's Café, Wayne and Lyle made plans. "Today is Friday, so we have the weekend to pack and get on the road," Wayne said. "Park your motorcycle in my shed and we can take my car."

"I have to leave my Dad a note telling him where I am," said Lyle, "he is working a construction job in Wisconsin Rapids and may not get home for a week."

"If we leave Sunday morning, we can be there by late afternoon. We cab meet at my house, have breakfast here and then be on our way."

The delivery van from Benbow's Appliance store was in the driveway that afternoon when Wayne arrived home. Two men were unloading the new washing machine.

"Take it right in the kitchen, then bring in the rinse tubs," Jan ordered.

"What did this new invention cost me?" Wayne asked. Jan handed him the bill.

"With the rinse tubs, which I gotta have, it comes to $25." Wayne handed her two tens and a five. Smiling and blushing, Jan looked as happy as a kitten with a new ball of yarn.

Over supper, Wayne told Jan about the job as a Deputy Sheriff and the training course at Camp McCoy.

"Don't you worry about a thing," she said, "just leave me some cash for expenses. You need new curtains for the bathroom, bedroom, and kitchen."

"Will $100 cover it?" Wayne asked with a smile.

"For that, I can get new drapes for the living room too and have money left over," Jan told him as she cut two slices of warm peach pie.

April in Wisconsin is an unpredictable month. Almost 60 degrees one day, snow the next, followed by rain then more sunshine. It was snowing lightly on the road to Camp McCoy. By the time Wayne and Lyle arrived, the sun was out. They checked in, got their training schedules, and were directed to the mess hall for supper. Eighteen other men were there from all over the state.

A state trooper greeted them, took their names, and said, "Grab a tray, get in line and find a seat." In the barracks, later hands were shook as introductions were made. Some were veterans from the war. Marines, Army, and Navy, all ready for a new adventure.

The two weeks seemed to fly by. A physical exam, classes on hand-to-hand combat, rifle, shotgun, and handgun practice, and a marksman competition, which Lyle won. Friends were made, phone numbers exchanged, and war experiences shared.

On the last day, everyone got a certificate from the state and a handshake from the Lieutenant Governor, who wished them well in their new law enforcement career. Wayne and Lyle got back to Marshfield around ten Saturday night. Lyle left for home on his motorcycle, and Wayne went straight to bed.

He awoke Sunday morning and got up to make coffee. The house smelled faintly of lemons and cinnamon. The new curtains brightened every room, and the new drapes had a roses and vines pattern. The kitchen cupboards were stocked with the basic needs, and the icebox held eggs, bacon, milk, and a covered dish of butter.

Outside, the sky was overcast with a damp wind. So, after coffee and a hot bath, Wayne laid out his suit, a white dress shirt, and a tie. The early service at the Lutheran church started at eight o'clock.

After the service, Wayne was greeted by several of his parent's friends. They asked how he was doing, invited him to dinner, and marveled that he had survived the dreaded flu. His father's friend, Emery Halverstadt, a teller at the bank, shook his hand. Emery had lost his wife, Eunice, and daughter Susan. It seemed everyone had lost someone in the family. Reverend Wilkey bid them all goodbye at the door.

Wayne and Lyle met at six o'clock Monday morning at Carson's cafe. Both were a little nervous but excited to begin a new adventure.

"Billy said to meet him at the office at seven," Wayne said.

"Just enough time for some pancakes," replied Lyle.

"Did you join the Military during the war?" Wayne asked.

Lyle nodded his head. "I joined the Navy in late September, 1918 and finished training at the Great Lakes Naval Academy in October. Before I could be posted to a ship, the Armistice was signed and the Navy let me and a thousand others go."

"You don't know how lucky you were," Wayne told him.

CHAPTER SEVEN

"Raise your right hands," Billy told them later that morning in his office. After they were sworn in, Billy handed them a Deputy Sheriff's badge and a map. "This is a plat map of Marshfield Township. Get familiar with it because it's the area you will be patrolling. Stop and talk to the landowners when you can."

He handed them each a brown paper-wrapped parcel. "I got you each a short-sleeved and long-sleeved uniform shirt with the Deputy patches already sewn on. You can wear your own pants."

From a desk drawer, Billy took out two web belts and holsters with flaps. An ammo pouch was attached. "As soon as possible, buy a leather ammo belt with loops. The holster will slide right on."

Wayne and Lyle strapped on and adjusted the web belts until they were comfortable. Then, reaching into the second drawer of the first file cabinet, Billy took out two pistols. Both were blued with a six-inch barrel and checkered walnut grips. Handing them over, he said softly, "You are now Deputy Sheriffs of Marshfield Township. Turning to Lyle, Billy said, "we have two cars right now, both 1917 Dodge sedans. I have one; you will patrol in the other." To Wayne, he said,

"I am meeting with the town board tomorrow morning. By next week I should have a patrol car for you. Until then, use yours and keep track of the mileage, so you get paid back."

Taking off the plaid hunting shirts they were wearing, Wayne and Lyle put on the tan long-sleeve uniform shirts. Adjusting their web belts, they looked at each other, and at that moment, it hit them. They were law enforcement officers, not just two town boys with a new job.

Billy watched them, remembering the same feeling he had many years ago. They would be responsible for the daily welfare of the people they were sworn to protect and those who made the decision to step outside the law. As if reading their minds, he opened another desk drawer and took out two sets of handcuffs with a small key attached to each. Handing each man a set, he said gruffly, "use them only if you have to."

Then he rose from behind the desk and unlocked the gun rack, removing two pump-action shotguns. Handing them to Wayne and Lyle, he told them, "you are each issued a Model 97 Winchester 12 gauge shotgun, to be used only in an emergency. I know both of your families, so I know you are familiar with this firearm and the damage it can do. One more thing before you go on patrol, stop at the photography studio and get your picture taken. The newspaper will print them. I want people to know who you are."

The day was warming up. It would be May next week, and the buds on the trees and bushes were opening up. The winter wheat crops were showing nicely, and wildflowers peeked through the green grass. However, Wayne's thoughts were not on the weather; he was thinking of Cassie Anderson.

She would be home in a week, and he was anxious to see her. He remembered her laugh and smile, her habit of winking at him like they were sharing a secret, and her light blonde, almost white hair, blue eyes, and slender figure. Then, right in the middle of his daydream, two deer stepped into the road in front of his car. He hit the clutch and brake and skidded to a dusty stop sideways in the road. The deer stared at him for a moment, then gracefully leaped into the ditch and strolled away.

'Better keep my mind on what I'm doing,' Wayne thought. About a mile later, a farmer on a tractor waited in a driveway for him to pass. They waved at each other as Wayne drove by.

Just before noon, Wayne saw the sign DARYL'S DINER. 'Good time to meet some local businessman,' he thought. He steered the Studebaker into the small dirt parking lot and stepped out, noting two other cars in the lot. An older Packard and a Model T flatbed truck. A small bell over the door jingled as he entered. Two men sat at the counter. The one slightly overweight and going bald wore a rumpled suit. 'Salesman,' thought Wayne.

The other was lean, wearing bib overalls and a worn gray shirt frayed at the elbows. 'Farmer,' Wayne decided. He sat at a table by the window where he could see his car. A well-developed young woman, about 19 or 20, with dark hair and freckles, walked up to take his order.

Looking him over carefully, she said, "I'm Edna, you must be new here,"

"Yes I am, and I'm hungry. How about a coffee, ham and cheese sandwich and some home fries."

Edna wrote it down and disappeared into the kitchen. Soon, an older man came out, wiping his hands on an apron. Stepping up to Wayne's table he held out his hand.

"I'm Daryl Weber," he said, "me and my wife Patti own the place. My daughter is the waitress." Then, pointing at Wayne's badge, he smiled and said, "Billy finally got him a Deputy."

"He got two," Wayne said with a grin. The two men shook hands, and Wayne told Daryl about Lyle. Edna bought his food and coffee, and Daryl returned to the kitchen. The salesman paid and left, and the farmer soon after. A quiet lunch in a quiet diner. 'Probably never happen again,' thought Wayne.

The rest of the day passed uneventfully. Taking backroads and hitting the occasional dead end, Wayne got a good idea of the layout of the territory. Tomorrow he and Lyle would switch, and soon they both would be familiar with the area. 'Hope he found some good eating places,' thought Wayne.

The sun was setting when Wayne got back to town. He met Lyle refueling at the Standard Gasoline pumps outside Snuffy's Garage. "You boys sure do look pretty in those new shirts," Snuffy said with a big grin.

"We also got new underwear," said Lyle, "want to see that too?"

"I'll pass on that," laughed Snuffy, then he turned serious. Be careful out there. It ain't all gonna be easy like today."

Billy greeted them at the office, took their reports, and sent them home.

CHAPTER EIGHT

Walking in the front door, Wayne smelled the delicious aroma of fried chicken. "Take your boots off in the entryway! I just mopped the floor and hallway," Jan yelled. After removing his boots, Wayne walked into the kitchen as Jan set down a cup of coffee.

"Fried chicken, potato wedges, and stewed tomatoes tonight," she beamed. The faint odor of soap and bleach flitted through the room. Looking out the kitchen window, the sight of a fully-loaded clothesline greeted him.

"I washed some of my work clothes with yours, hope you don't mind," Jan said with a slight blush on her cheeks.

"I don't mind one bit," Wayne said with a little chuckle, "we have got to break in that new washing machine, make it pay for itself." They both started laughing until they had to sit down. Wayne thought, 'as long as Jan is working here, each day will be a new adventure.'

Saturday, May 3rd, dawned warm and sunny with a light breeze. The rose bushes around the front porch began to show petals. Jan had hired some local boys to mow the lawn and dig the garden plot. The maple tree was in full leaf and would soon offer shade from the summer sun.

The train from Minneapolis would be arriving at ten this morning, bringing Cassie back home. Wayne had the day off and would drive Helen Anderson to the station to pick her up. Billy would be home at noon. Sitting on the porch swing with his morning coffee,

Wayne nervously drummed his fingers on the arm of the swing. 'Why am I jittery?' he wondered. 'No reason to be, just meeting an old friend.' He thought back to the last time he had talked to her. The conversation had been tense as Cassie wanted to know why he had enlisted.

'The U.S. Army has enough soldiers, they won't miss you if you stay home.' They had argued about honor and duty. Finally, she told him she was going to nursing school in Minneapolis.

'We were sitting on this very swing when she stormed off, her cheeks red with anger,' Wayne thought. Just then, two mourning doves flew in and lit on the lowest branch of the maple. *Good sign,* Wayne thought, *a very good sign.*

The train was right on time. Gray smoke puffed from the stack as it slowly eased up to the platform. Then, with a hissing of steam, it came to a stop, and the engineer throttled back. The conductors opened the doors, and people slowly began emerging. Cassie was the last person to leave the second car. She was smiling, but her face was pale and drawn.

Her mother wrapped her in a hug, gently patting her back. Letting her go, Helen motioned Wayne closer. Cassie looked him over with tired eyes, smiled, and said, "I could use another hug." Wayne put his arms around his friend. What Wayne felt was not something he could put into words, but he was sure Cassie felt it too. They fit together. When she let him go, she was blushing slightly, and her eyes held a new light, like an awakening.

Stepping back, Wayne said, "I'll get your bags and put them in the car."

Cassie took her mother's arm. "Where's dad?"

"Take one guess," said Helen.

"He will be home for lunch," Cassie said with a little laugh.

Driving along the northern boundary of their patrol area, Lyle was smiling to himself. He had just had lunch at Daryl's Diner and met Edna Weber. They had hit it off right away. 'Those freckles are sure cute,' Lyle thought, 'and the hazel eyes don't let you go.'

Off the county road to his right, the Little Eau Pleine river could be seen through the trees. A Model T Ford was parked in a turnaround. As Lyle slowed to look at the auto, two men came up the path from the river. Both carried cane poles; one had a bait bucket, the other a half-gallon jug. The larger of the two staggered slightly and laughed. The smaller one saw Lyle first and stopped. He said something to his friend, who also stopped and looked at Lyle's car.

'Homemade whiskey in the jug,' Lyle thought as he got out of the car. As he watched them slowly move toward him, he guessed the bigger one weighed maybe 200 lbs., was about six feet tall, and already going to fat. The jug he carried was half empty. The smaller one would be around five ft. 8 inches and weigh maybe 150 lbs. 'Same dark hair, same features, must be brothers,' Lyle thought. Thumbing back his hat, Lyle asked, "Anything biting today?"

"None of your damn business," said the big one. Taking

a step closer, he looked Lyle up and down. "You the new Deputy we heard about," he said, "I don't like Deputies."

"Once you get to know me, you might change your mind," Lyle said as he moved sideways away from the car to keep both men in sight. The smaller man set down his cane pole and bait bucket and sat on the ground with his arms around his knees, grinning. The bigger man dropped his pole and the jug when his eyes fixed on Lyle's badge.

"Always wanted me a shiny Deputy badge," he said and reached for Lyle's shirt with his right hand. Lyle blocked him with his left forearm, grabbed his shirt with his left hand, and pulled him close, driving a knee into the man's crotch. The big man folded with an 'oof' and rolled on the ground. The small man turned pal, but didn't move.

Lyle pulled his notebook from his back pocket and asked him, "what are your names?" They were brothers, Louis and Joe Gandt. Louis, the big one, was still trying to get to his feet without much luck. "Where did you get the whiskey," Lyle asked Joe.

"Louis stole it from Pa's truck," Joe said, "I don't know where Pa got it."

Lyle took down their address and let them go. 'I don't think I have seen the last of Louis Gandt,' he thought.

The Anderson's sat down to supper that night, a family together again. "When do you start work at the hospital," Billy asked Cassie.

"I have a week off and start on Monday, May 12th," Cassie said.

"Will you need an auto right away," Helen asked.

"Not really," said Cassie, "I can walk a block over to Chestnut St. and take the trolley car; it goes right by the hospital."

Billy told them about Lyle's meeting with the Gandt boys.

"I remember Louis Gandt," Cassie said, "he was always a bully."

"It runs in the family," Billy said, "their father Rodney was the same. I got a suspicion he may be running a whiskey still back in his woods. No real evidence yet, just a gut feeling."

"My boy is hurt real bad," the farmer told Wayne. It was Monday morning about five miles south of Marshfield. On his regular patrol, Wayne had almost passed the farm driveway when he saw the man come running from the barn. As he pulled into the drive, the farmer, Earl Duchow, ran up to the car and yelled through the open window, "We need help!"

Wayne stopped by the barn and got out of the car. "What happened?"

With tears in his eyes, Earl said, "that young bull got loose, broke right out of his stanchion. Lucas tried to get a rope on him and the bull gored him in the side!"

Young Lucas was lying on hay bales while his mother, Lydia, tended his wound. Kneeling, Wayne took Lydia firmly but gently by the shoulder.

"Get a clean dishtowel to cover the wound. Also we have to wrap something around him to hold the towel in place."

"I've got an old bed sheet I was gonna cut up for rags," Lydia said, "we'll tear it into strips and wrap him good."

When Lucas was bandaged, Wayne and Earl got him into the backseat of Wayne's car with Lydia. Wayne drove to the hospital in Marshfield with Earl following in his truck.

As a doctor and a nurse took the boy inside, Lydia came back, gave Wayne a motherly hug, kissed his cheek, and followed her son. Wayne drove to the office and wrote out a report for Billy.

"Good thing you were there," Billy said, "you did just right." Then, shuffling some papers, Billy pulled one loose and handed it to Wayne. "Got the approval from the town board for another patrol car. Go see Harry Mason and pick out a decent vehicle; maybe take Snuffy with you."

"Just took in a 1918 Dodge sedan," Harry said, "old Doc Teasedale traded it for a new Cadillac." Snuffy had the hood open, inspecting the engine. Then he crawled under the Dodge, sliding on his back from the front to the rear.

Standing back up with a smile, Snuffy said, "I'm taking it for a test drive." Harry handed him the key. Snuffy was back in ten minutes. "It needs a new oil-pan seal, plugs, and oil change." Then, turning to Wayne, he said, "it's got some hard miles on it. With new tires it's worth $250."

Harry nodded his head. "Take it, and have the board send me the check.

"Put the new tires in the back," said Snuffy, "I'll put them on after I do the tune-up."

Back at the office, Billy said, "I'll take the bill of sale to the board tonight. Snuffy's word is good enough for me."

CHAPTER NINE

Wayne stood staring into his closet, scratching his head. Jan stuck her head in the door and asked, "What do you want for supper?"

"I'm having supper at the Anderson's tonight," he said. "I'm just wondering what to wear."

"Well, it's a meal with old friends and their pretty daughter, so just dress casual." Jan said with a grin.

Blushing a little, Wayne said, "Cassie is just a friend too."

Slowly shaking her head, Jan said, "you young people spend too much time waltzing around each other. If you like her, which I think you do, tell her, then kiss her!"

"My God Jan," Wayne said with a slight gasp, "what if she slapped me?"

"Yeah, she might," Jan said with a big grin, "but what if she kissed you right back? At least you would know where you stand!"

"Alright, I'll dress casual," said Wayne.

The Andersons and Wayne ate in the dining room. The tablecloth and the linen napkins had been ironed. Billy had shaved and wore a white shirt. Helen served a baked ham with rings of pineapple and mashed potatoes, gravy, and fresh asparagus.

"We seldom get to use the dining room because of Billy's odd hours," Helen said.

Cassie looked lovely wearing a white and pink floral dress. "Mom had me ironing all afternoon," she said with a little grin. She wore her blonde hair shorter now and was getting a light tan. Wayne tried to act casual, wishing he had at least worn a tie.

"Snuffy brought the Dodge over this afternoon," Billy said, spearing another piece of ham. "I took it for a drive and it runs great."

"Now you each have an auto to patrol in," Helen said. "Would anyone like coffee?"

"How are things at the hospital?" Wayne asked Cassie.

"Not as many flu cases," she said. "It seems to have run its course. It's a miracle you survived Wayne, very few do."

"You work around it every day," Wayne told her. "I can't imagine the courage it must take to do that."

Cassie blushed. "God is looking over me just as he looked over you."

During this exchange, Helen and Billy were quiet, watching these two young people and sensing a bond being re-established.

Helen and Cassie cleared the table after the meal, and Cassie offered to help with the dishes.

"Your father will help with the dishes," Helen said. "Why don't you and Wayne take a walk, it's a lovely evening. Take a sweater, it may get cooler later."

"Do you think my parents are trying to get us together?" Cassie asked as they walked.

"I do get that feeling and I have missed your company. We used to talk all the time about everything."

Cassie slipped her arm through his. "I think we maybe got too close, taking each other for granted. I've missed having you around."

"I thought of you often while I was in France," Wayne said softly. "I wrote you once, but didn't know where to send it."

"I didn't want you to join the Army because I was afraid for you," Cassie admitted. "I was afraid you would get hurt or even die alone in some foreign country." A silence settled over them, each deep in their own thoughts, hoping the other would say the right thing, make the first move.

The sun had set, and the shadows of the evening slowly eased out the light. Finally, they stopped walking, and Wayne turned Cassie to face him. "I'm going to kiss you," he said, "and I'm hoping you won't slap me."

Cassie smiled wistfully. "I won't slap you. In fact, I may kiss you back." Slowly and softly, they kissed their first kiss together, his arms around her back, hers around his neck. Then, slowly and gently, they parted, both stunned by the feeling.

"Why did we wait so long?" they said together, then laughed. They walked on, talking and stopping now and then to kiss again. A new chapter in their lives was unfolding, and they welcomed it.

Wayne arrived at the office the next morning smiling and cheerful.

"You sure are in a good mood this morning," Lyle said. "Must have been a good dinner last night."

"I'll tell you about it later," Wayne said. "Have you met Edna Weber at the diner yet?"

"As a matter of fact, we have a date for Friday night. She wants to go see a moving picture at the old Opera House."

"What time does it start? Maybe I might ask Cassie to go."

"Ask Cassie to go where?" asked Billy as he walked in the door.

"To a moving picture show at the Opera House," Wayne answered.

"I'm sure she would like it," Billy nodded, "but right now, get out on patrol. The Marshfield police want us to be on the lookout for a Cadillac stolen in Spencer last night. It belongs to a Judge, and he wants it back."

Curtis Yonke had never driven such a fine automobile. He had been walking from Colby that evening, hoping for a ride, but no one stopped. When he passed the judge's office in Spencer, the bright new Cadillac parked there seemed to call out to him. Slowly, Curtis eased his skinny five ft. 9-inch frame into the driver's seat. That was all it took. In less than a minute, he was on his way to Marshfield.

As he piloted the big auto down the highway, he glanced at the gauges on the dashboard. The gas tank was almost empty! He would need to fuel up, but the only money he had was the nickel he found the day before. 'One of these farmers must have some gas,' he thought.

He drove slowly, watching for just the right place. Finally, he found a farmhouse with only one light on and the big fuel tank standing between the barn and machine shed, back-lit by the three-quarter moon. Sneaking through the field, he made his way to the big tank. Two gas cans sat beneath the tank—a one-gallon and a big five-gallon. He quietly checked the cans. Both were empty. There was a slight rattling noise as he unhooked the nozzle and began filling the larger can. All of a sudden, a dog started barking from the porch.

'Time to go,' thought Curtis. He dropped the gas nozzle, grabbed the can, and ran down the driveway with the half-full canister bumping against his knee. The dog caught him halfway down the drive, grabbed a mouthful of pants-leg, and held on. Curtis stumbled and fell, which probably saved him when the farmer fired his shotgun.

BOOM!

The gas can went flying as Curtis kicked at the dog with his free leg, sending it rolling away from him. He made it to the Cadillac and took off in a shower of gravel. Three miles later, the Cadillac gave a few coughs and stopped—out of gas. Curtis left it there and raced away, just glad to be alive.

The next morning, Lyle found the Cadillac abandoned, out of gas, but otherwise undamaged. The farmer, Elias Berndt, had called to report a gasoline thief. He told Lyle about the dog barking and the chase down the drive, totally forgetting to mention the shotgun blast. The dented gas can and the piece of denim the dog proudly bought back confirmed the story. Using the farmer's phone, he called Snuffy, who towed the auto to Marshfield, where the Judge later claimed it.

CHAPTER TEN

Helen Anderson had hoped the dinner and the walk later would bring Cassie and Wayne together. Her hopes were realized the next morning when Cassie came down to breakfast. Billy had eaten early after getting a phone call about a stolen car. Cassie was dressed in her nurse's uniform, and Helen caught a slight whiff of perfume. Cassie seemed to have more spirit, more purpose than the day before.

"Did you and Wayne have a nice walk last night?" she asked.

Cassie smiled. "It wasn't just nice, it was wonderful. He kissed me, and I kissed him back. It was the first time we ever kissed each other."

A tear formed at the corner of Helen's eye. "I've known for a long time that you two belonged together. Now, you know it too."

"So much has happened since the war, we need to talk about it and share all that happened when we were apart," Cassie said. With a quick hug, Cassie was out the door and off to work.

The Old Opera House was once the most popular place for miles around. It was built right after the Civil War and took three years to complete. Many of the great opera stars of that age had graced the hardwood stage. Plush velvet curtains adorned the backdrop, with all the seats padded with the same fine cloth.

It closed its doors in 1915 and sat empty until March of 1919 when an enterprising couple, Franklin and Collette Neuman, re-opened it as a moving picture house. A huge white backdrop took the place of the velvet drapes, and a film projector was mounted in the lower balcony above the main entrance. Franklin ran the projector, and Collette played the piano sitting to the right of the screen upon entry.

Wayne and Cassie met Lyle and Edna at the door. Cassie and Edna hit it off right away. Cassie hugged Lyle. They had been in the same group all through school.

"I've never seen one of these, what's it like?" Wayne asked.

"It's so exciting," Edna said. "Sometimes sad, sometimes funny and sometimes there is a lot of action."

The house was about half-full as the four found their seats. The lights dimmed, and the projector began a whirring sound as Franklin turned it on. Collette began the piano music as the credits rolled onto the screen. The film was titled 'When the clouds roll by,' starring Douglas Fairbanks. It was a comedy/drama that ran for 90 minutes. After the film, the two couples parted, Lyle and Edna speeding off on the motorcycle.

On the drive home, neither Wayne nor Cassie were ready to talk of the past year. Instead, he asked about her day at the hospital, and she wanted to hear how his day on patrol went. They needed this time to be close again, test their boundary limits, and feel comfortable opening their hearts to a new experience. It would take time, but they were young, and time favors the young.

The Women's Temperance League was having a march down Main Street. It was a show of support for what was known as the Volstead Act, the 18th Amendment to the U.S. Constitution prohibiting the sale and transportation of alcohol. The ladies assembled at the northern end of Main St. about 100 strong, with the High School band leading the way. They had banners to be carried and held high, many waved small flags at the crowd, and one brawny woman in a large hat shouted through a megaphone. Some bystanders cheered, some booed, and some just shook their heads.

Was this really a good idea? Breweries and taverns would go out of business! What about wine for the church's religious ceremonies? Many farmers grew grain for the breweries; what about them? Everyone had questions, few had answers. Every State had ratified the Amendment except Rhode Island, and in January of 1920, it would become the law of the land.

Irene Boetcher had called the Sheriff's office about a trespasser. As Wayne drove up to the farm, he saw the husband, Melvin Boetcher, arguing with a woman. Taking his notepad, Wayne went to investigate.

The short, stout woman was holding a basket half-full of asparagus. "What seems to be the trouble?" Wayne asked.

"This woman is stealing my asparagus," said Melvin, "and I want it back."

"This asparagus is growing wild in the ditch," the woman shouted. "The ditch is part of the road, which belongs to the county, so I ain't stealing, I'm harvesting!"

Wayne held up his hands. "Both of you be quiet a minute and let me think." Then, turning to Melvin, he asked, "Who mows the grass along the side of the road in the summer?"

"I do," said Melvin, "for two miles, on both sides."

Turning to the woman, Wayne said, "Since Melvin is not paid in cash for the mowing, he is entitled to what grows wild in the ditch."

"I never heard of such a thing," the stout woman gasped, "now what do we do?" Reaching into the basket, Wayne removed about half the asparagus and handed it to Melvin. "I think you need to find another place to get your wild asparagus," Wayne told the woman.

Eyes blazing and chin held high, the woman climbed out of the ditch and stormed down the road. Melvin looked down at the asparagus in his hand, nodded, and looked up at Wayne. "Thanks, I guess," he mumbled and walked down his drive to the house. Wayne noted the incident, got into his car, and went back on patrol.

Lyle's day was not going well. The gravel road along the Little Eau Pleine river was a nice enough drive until a piece of barbed wire found a resting place in the rear tire of the Dodge patrol car. Getting out the jack, Lyle jacked up the rear end and removed the flat, putting on the spare tire. As he was finishing up, a Pierce-Arrow touring car with two men inside drove up, stopped, and honked their horn.

"Get that piece of junk out of the road," yelled the red-faced fat man at the wheel. The tall, lanky man beside him raised a half-gallon jug to his mouth and drank. Both wore white straw hats; the fat man wore glasses.

'Couple of drunks,' thought Lyle. "Be out of your way in a minute," Lyle called back. Then, putting the flat tire in the back of the Dodge and tossing the jack on the back floor, he approached the big touring car. The tall, lanky man was having trouble focusing on Lyle. His blurred gaze took in the badge on Lyle's shirt.

"He's a deputy Alvin," he slurred. Red-faced Alvin grabbed the jug and hugged it to his chest.

"He ain't taking our whiskey, Nicky," he told his friend.

"Where did you two gentlemen get the whiskey?" Lyle asked.

"We ain't 'genelmen,' and we ain't telling," said Nicky. Lyle reached across Nicky to take the jug from Alvin, and Nicky punched him in the chest. It was a glancing blow, without much force due to Nicky's condition, but now the situation changed. Lyle yanked Nicky out of the car, threw him down on the ground, and cuffed him. Nicky lay there, too stunned to even roll over. Alvin let out a yell, climbed out of the Pierce-Arrow, and weaved his way around the car, swinging his fists.

Lyle slowly backed up as Alvin stumbled toward him. Focusing on Lyle, Alvin forgot about Nicky on the ground and tripped over him, falling face down across his friend. Lyle dropped with his knee on Alvin's back and grabbed Alvin's right arm, bringing it up behind his back. Using the belt from his pants, Lyle soon had Alvin subdued.

While lying on the ground, Alvin started to snore. Lyle took the belt off and half-dragged, half-carried the man to the rear seat of the touring car. Lyle took the handcuffs off of Nicky and asked again, "Where did you get the whiskey?"

Nicky had sobered enough to follow the question. "At the turnaround about five miles back, a chubby guy named Louis sold Alvin that jug for a dollar.

'Louis Gandt,' thought Lyle. 'Sheriff Billy is not going to like this.'

"Can you drive?" Lyle asked Nicky.

"If you turn it around for me, I can drive right home," said Nicky. Lyle got the car turned around, and watched Nicky drive slowly away with Alvin asleep in the back.

Sheriff Billy Anderson sat on the running board of his Dodge, watching a farmer cutting first-crop hay using a McCormick tractor. 'I miss the horses,' thought Billy. His father had farmed his entire life with horses; now, tractors did most of the work. Sure, the work went faster, but the noise echoed across the fields as the big steel-wheeled machines chewed up the land.

A few of the old-timers still used a horse and buggy to go to town or church, but each week there seemed to be less of them. Many farms had buggies parked next to machine sheds with weeds growing up through the wheels. Slowly shaking his head, Billy climbed into his patrol car and drove away.

CHAPTER ELEVEN

On June 10th, 1919, the Marshfield news carried the headline: STATE RATIFIES 19TH AMENDMENT! Known as the women's Suffrage bill, the state of Wisconsin supported the right of women to vote in all state and national elections. The telephone lines in Marshfield were tied up for hours as the news spread. The men just nodded their heads, saying 'it was bound to happen' and 'hope they use it wisely.' Politicians were busy rewriting speeches to include the new voters. Women could now run for office in state elections, and some were planning to do so.

"How much chicken do you want me to fry?" yelled Jan from the kitchen. Wayne came in from the back door carrying a wood crate of soft drinks.

"For the four of us, probably two chickens should do it," he said. It was Sunday morning, and Wayne and Cassie were going on a picnic in the park with Lyle and Edna.

"What else do you need?" Jan asked.

"Edna is bringing potato salad, Cassie is making coleslaw and Lyle is bringing dessert. He didn't say what kind."

Jan pointed with a big fork at the kitchen table. "In that box are plates, napkins, a tablecloth, silverware and serving spoons. You be sure to bring them all back when the picnic is done."

Wayne laughed. "You think of everything!"

With a big grin, Jan said, "As your housekeeper, that's my job."

It was a picture-perfect June Sunday. Scattered white puffy clouds floated around the bright sun. Laughing and shouting children could be heard having fun on the playground. Wayne and Lyle unloaded the food from the auto as Cassie and Edna spread the tablecloth on one of the new picnic tables.

"I love these new dresses," Edna said, "they are so comfortable."

Both girls wore the new women's style. No more floor-length dresses. The new style was short-sleeved, open-neck summer wear that stopped just below the knee.

"My dad almost had a fit when he first saw the new style," Cassie said, "but mom says she is going to get some new dresses too."

"I like the new style," said Lyle, "those long dresses hid the natural beauty of women."

"Men's knickers are almost a thing of the past," Wayne said, "those buckles just below the knee always tore my long socks."

Reaching into the wood case on the ground, Lyle pulled out a bottle. "Who wants a root beer?" he asked.

As they ate, the four young people talked and planned. Things were happening in the world. In April, a young man named Leslie Irvin made the first free-fall parachute jump. In Winnipeg, Manitoba, Canada, a city-wide workers strike shut down the city. John Alcock and Arthur Brown had just completed the first non-stop trans-Atlantic flight, taking off from New Jersey and landing in County Galway, Ireland.

"I would love to go up in an airplane," said Edna, "It must be so exciting."

"There is talk of mail being flown across the country," Lyle said, "imagine someone getting a letter the day after you mail it."

"Automobile racing is big now," Wayne said. "Louis Chevrolet is building a race car that he says will do 120 miles per hour."

"A company in England is building an airship that will be filled with a special kind of gas," Cassie said, "and they are going to float across the Atlantic to New York City."

"Remember the first trolley-car in Marshfield?" Lyle added. "My dad helped lay the tracks right down Main Street. Now we just take it for granted."

It was late afternoon when the four parted, Lyle and Edna roaring off on the Indian motorcycle. The leftovers, linens, and dishes went in the back of Wayne's Studebaker.

"Before I take you home, let's drop all this off at my house," Wayne said, "and you can meet my housekeeper, Jan."

"Mom told me all about Jan," said Cassie. "I would love to meet her."

"Did you save me some chicken?" Jan asked as Wayne carried the big napkin-wrapped basket into the kitchen, followed by Cassie with the box of dishes and silverware.

"Hi Jan, I'm Cassie," she said, "and that was the most delicious chicken ever."

Jan smiled and blushed. "I'm so glad you liked it; maybe one night Wayne will invite you over for my mushroom and onion pork chops."

"That sounds delicious," Cassie said. "You can eat with us as our chaperone."

"I hate this work," Floyd Krause told his friend Morgan Novak. The two young men had just finished digging a deep hole for a two-seater outhouse. Floyd was average everything: five-foot-nine, tall, lean, with dark hair. Morgan looked about the same, a little heavier in the middle with light brown hair. They had been hired two weeks earlier by Gene Rittenhouse Construction Inc. to learn the home building business.

"This is how I started my business," Gene had told them. Sitting on top of the pile of dirt, they drank from the canteen of water.

"It's a hard way to make $15 a week, Floyd," whined Morgan wiping his sweat away.

"At least it's Friday; we get paid today."

By ten that evening, both had drunk and gambled away their pay at the Red Rooster Tavern in Stetsonville. Then, weaving their way through the parking lot, Morgan stopped to admire a new Packard sedan.

"Sure would like to have a car like this someday," he slurred to his friend.

Floyd opened the door to the passenger side and looked inside. "I bet this car can do a hundred miles an hour." Then, without thinking, Floyd opened the glove box. Inside lay a revolver. Taking it out, Floyd almost drooled as he held it in his hand. It was a Smith & Wesson double-action blue steel six-shot .38 special.

"Let's take the gun and go," Morgan said nervously, but Floyd had a better idea.

"Let's take the car too."

"What if we get caught," Morgan whined.

"Then we get free room and board in jail." Floyd laughed. "Beats digging outhouse holes." They started the Packard and slowly rolled out of the parking lot with Floyd at the wheel.

They slept in the car that night, parked in a dilapidated old barn a few miles outside of town. Waking up, Morgan had a headache and misgivings about riding around in a stolen auto. He was not a criminal and didn't wish to become one. From the backseat, he sat up slowly and looked into the front seat where Floyd was on his back, softly snoring. Morgan quietly opened the rear door, set his hat firmly on his aching head, and walked out the rear of the barn. He decided that walking down the road was a bad idea since the police were probably looking for the Packard. Morgan set out across the hayfield, disappearing into history.

An hour later, Floyd awoke, sat up groggily, and looked around for Morgan, who was long gone. Nestled against his leg was the revolver. Picking it up, he popped open the cylinder, saw it was fully loaded with six shiny shells, and snapped it closed. Floyd began planning his day. The gasoline gauge read three-quarters full.

'Got to head south, maybe Milwaukee,' he thought, 'rob some small town banks on the way for spending money.' Sticking the gun in his belt, Floyd backed the car out of the barn, turned around, and drove south.

CHAPTER TWELVE

Billy hung up the telephone Saturday morning when Wayne and Lyle walked into the office. "I want the two of you patrolling together today," he said. "A Packard sedan was stolen in Stetsonville last night, probably headed this way." The telephone rang, and Billy answered. Grabbing a notepad, he wrote something down and hung up.

"The Savings & Loan in Abbotsford was just robbed. A teller says the man drove off in a big Packard, and went south on Highway 13."

It had almost been too easy. Floyd drove into the parking lot of the Savings & Loan just as the manager was unlocking the door. Pulling the revolver from his belt, he ordered the man inside.

"Just give me what you got in the drawer," Floyd demanded. "Just the bills, no coins." Stuffing the money in his shirt, Floyd backed out the door, got in the car, and drove off.

Wayne and Lyle drove slowly north on Highway 13, watching for the stolen Packard. Traffic was light on a Saturday morning, some Model Ts, a few Chevrolets, even a wagon pulled by a team of horses.

"He must have stopped somewhere," Lyle said. "Maybe for gasoline." Then they saw it. Coming toward them, the driver passed without slowing down or speeding up. Wayne drove into the nearest driveway, turned around, and gave chase.

Floyd stopped in a diner in Spencer for coffee and breakfast. The hangover was fading, and his stomach had been growling for the last five miles. With a pocket full of money, Floyd ordered eggs, bacon, potatoes, sausage, and toast.

'Haven't seen a police car all morning,' he wondered. He finished the coffee, paid the bill, and left. The gasoline gauge told him he still had a half-tank of fuel. Then, he saw the Dodge stop. In his rearview mirror, he watched it turn around and come after him.

'Let's see if they can keep up with this Packard,' he thought with a smile. When his speedometer read 75, he was roaring down the Main Street of Marshfield with the Dodge right behind him. Then, around the long curve by Phillip's Drugstore, Floyd's luck ran out. The trolley car was coming right at him!

Wayne was keeping up with the Packard but not gaining much.

"Slow down, slow down," Lyle shouted. "That crazy fool is going to run head-on into the trolley!"

CRASH!

Wayne braked, running it up on the curb and knocking over baskets of produce outside Miller's Market. Getting out of their car, Lyle and Wayne ran over to the Packard. Floyd lay half in and half out of where the windshield had been. The steering wheel had bent sideways when Floyd's chest had slammed into it. Floyd was dead. No human could have lived through that crash.

The Marshfield police came running to the scene. "Get a doctor!" one of them hollered. The trolley car had been pushed back about five feet with no other real damage other than a big dent in the front. One of the women on board had banged her head on the seat; otherwise, no one inside was hurt.

An Ambulance arrived, removing Floyd from the car and taking him to the morgue. Snuffy arrived with his tow truck and hauled the Packard to his garage. Sheriff Billy called the Stetsonville police to let them know about the wreck. What money was found on Floyd be returned to the Savings & Loan in Abbotsford. The Smith & Wesson revolver was found jammed under the dashboard of the Packard, still fully loaded. Having no known relatives, Floyd's body would be buried at the lower end of the Episcopal cemetery, a spot reserved for unclaimed corpses.

After Wayne and Lyle wrote their report for Billy, a reporter was waiting to talk to them.

"How many times did you shoot at him?"

We never fired a shot," Wayne said. "And he never shot at us. We were too busy driving."

The reporter looked sad. "Shooting always makes a better story."

Lyle stopped at Daryl's Diner after work and told Edna about the crash. "I don't think he even knew Marshfield had a trolley," Lyle said. "He just plowed right into it."

"I'm just glad you and Wayne didn't get hurt," Edna told him.

"Wayne is an excellent driver— managed to brake and get out of the way," Lyle said.

Daryl walked out of the kitchen and patted Lyle on the shoulder. "Maybe this will be a lesson for someone else not to speed through town."

The first crop hat was cut and in the hay-mows by the end of June. Now people were getting ready for the Fourth of July. Merchants hung bunting and banners up and down Main Street. Flags decorated every lamppost and telephone pole. Men and women alike wore white straw hats with red and blue bands. A town picnic was planned for the park, and The Loyal Order of Elks would sponsor a parade down Main Street.

With the great War now over and the Spanish flu in remission, people were ready to celebrate. A bandstand with a podium was being built in the park center where the Mayor, Elmer J. Bainbridge, would make a lengthy speech about 143 years in the land of plenty.

"Lyle will stop traffic on the north end of town at noon," Sheriff Billy explained, "Wayne will do the same on the south end."

"How long do we hold up traffic?" Wayne asked.

"A city policeman will let you know when to let cars through," Billy said. "The parade should take about a half-hour, with a little time at the end to get them all off Main Street."

"Who will be on patrol?" Lyle asked.

Billy leaned back in his chair and smiled. "No patrol on the 4th. After the parade, spend the day with your sweethearts and have fun."

CHAPTER THIRTEEN

The vendors had taken over the north end of the park. The food vendors had hot dogs, burgers, bratwurst, fried chicken, and a variety of salads. Ice cream was available in three flavors, vanilla, chocolate, and strawberry. Souvenirs of all kinds, from statues to sleeve garters and postcards. Four polka bands took turns playing throughout the day, and a dance floor was in constant use. Even the portly mayor took a turn around the floor.

About three o'clock in the afternoon, Wayne and Cassie found a quiet bench by the creek to rest. "I am so glad that Dad gave you and Lyle the day off," Cassie said, "I've been wanting to talk to you about us."

Taking her hand in his, Wayne said, "There are some things I have been wanting to tell you also. I thought of you often while I was in France. I carried your picture all through the war."

Cassie laid her head on Wayne's shoulder. "At nursing school, I met a doctor, David Blake. I was very attracted to him, and when he asked me to marry him, I said yes." Raising her head, Cassie brushed away the tear from her eye. "I didn't realize it then, but I do now," she said softly. "I was attracted to him because he reminded me so much of you."

Lifting her chin slightly with his hand, Wayne kissed Cassie. It was the tender kiss of young lovers, lips slightly parted, breathing the essence of each other. As they slowly parted, each knew they had found the love they had longed for.

The celebration lasted until dusk. The vendors packed up and left. The polka bands bid farewell and the people began slowly making their way home. Old friendships had been renewed and new friends made. Wayne and Cassie, hand in hand, caught up with Lyle and Edna, also hand in hand, near the park entrance.

"I'm glad it's Friday," Lyle said. "We will need the weekend to recover from all the fun."

It was four blocks from the park to the Anderson house. Wayne and Cassie strolled slowly, arm in arm talking and planning. "Jan says I need some new furniture," Wayne said. "I would like it if you helped her pick out just the right stuff."

"Your living room could use a new coat of paint also," Cassie said with a smile.

With a sigh, Wayne conceded. "First the paint, then the furniture."

Cassie giggled. "As long as the living room is getting new paint, let's do the dining room too."

"Don't forget the kitchen. Jan will help you pick out the colors." Wayne laughed.

By noon Saturday, the town was back to normal. People had been busy all morning cleaning up the park and taking down flags and banners. Wayne and Lyle had left early on patrol and met at Daryl's Diner for lunch. The diner was half-full of customers when they entered.

Taking the corner booth, they waited for Edna. A big man at the counter eating a sandwich watched them. Edna came by with a big smile and took their order. As she walked away, the big man stood up from his stool and walked over to them. His bib-overalls were stained and dirty, his under-shirt faded and torn.

"You the new deputies that been bothering my boys," he said with a growl.

"And who might you be?" Wayne asked.

"I'm Rodney Gandt. And if you know what's good for you, leave me and my boys be."

"As long as you and your sons stay out of trouble, we have no interest in you," Lyle told him.

"My boy Louis says you hit him when he wasn't looking," Rodney said with a sneer.

"Louis was too drunk to see much of anything," Lyle said. "And your other son, Joe, said Louis got the whiskey from you." Rodney backed up a step, shuffled his feet a bit and walked out of the Diner.

It was late afternoon when Wayne saw a sight that was to be repeated many times over for years to come—a McCormick tractor buried in a mud hole. The left rear wheel was a quarter of the way in the mud, and the right wheel had sunk to the hub. Two four-horse teams strained mightily, but the tractor barely moved. Another four-horse hitch was added, and slowly the tractor emerged from the hole. It looked for all the world as if Mother earth had given a difficult birth to a machine. The farmers laughed, shook hands all around and the horses were led away.

Wayne and Lyle reported their conversation with Rodney

Gandt to Sheriff Billy. "I think it might be time to put some revenue agents on Rodney's tail," Billy said with a smile. "It probably won't stop him completely, but it will sure slow him down."

"Louis and Joe like to hang out by the river," Lyle said. "They could lead agents right to the still."

Rubbing his chin, Billy said, "Rumors have been circulating for years about the Gandt's still. In fact, people say there are three stills, two small ones and a big one. The small ones are decoys. We want the big one." Stepping over to the county map, Billy pointed to a spot. "Claude Bettendorf's woodlot butts up against Gandt's property right here. Claude and Rodney don't get along, so Claude would have no problem if we set up a blind to keep an eye on Rodney. I'll talk to him tomorrow."

HOBART'S PAINT & WALLPAPER INC. read the sign on the side of the truck parked in the driveway when Wayne got home. Jan had the kitchen cleared of all the furniture, which now was stacked in the dining room.

"This will cover up that dingy brown paint and make the kitchen brighter," she said holding up a four inch square of a light yellow paper.

"I like it," said Wayne. "What colors for the dining and living rooms?"

"Got them right here," she said, and held up a light tan square and an off-white square. "The tan is for the living room, the white for the dining room."

"How did you decide on the colors?" Wayne asked.

"Cassie and I picked them out. She said you would like them."

"I do like them. So, how long will this job take?"

"A day for each room and I'll be here to make sure it's done right," Jan assured him.

"I guess I'll eat at the cafe tonight," he sighed.

"Cassie told me you were to eat at the Anderson's until the job is done," Jan said with a big smile.

CHAPTER FOURTEEN

Claude Bettendorf not only agreed to let Sheriff Billy on his land, he also helped to build the blind. "When the wind is right, I can smell that mash cooking," he said. "I hope you find it and bust it up good."

The blind sat back about 15 yards from the Gandt's property, flanked by blackberry brush and nettles. From inside, about 25 yards away, the bend of a much used trail could be seen meandering back into the woods.

"When you want to use it, park your car by my machine shed and just walk in," Claude said.

"If it's not me, it will be one of my deputies," said Billy, "I'll make a little map for each of them to follow."

AGRICULTURE SECRETARY COMING TO MARSHFIELD! Was the headline in the Marshfield news. This was big news for Wisconsin farmers. Wayne and Lyle were having an early breakfast at Carson's Cafe. Wayne had bought a paper on his way in and showed Lyle the headline.

"When is this politician due to arrive?" asked Lyle.

"It says his train will take him to Madison on Monday, July 21st, then he will be in Marshfield by noon on the 23rd. His name is David F. Houston."

"What does he plan to do while he is here?" Lyle asked.

Wayne chuckled. "My guess is he'll make a speech in the park about what a great job he's doing, ask people to re-elect Wilson next year, then get back on the train and go home."

"With prohibition coming, farmers are going to be hard hit, " Lyle said. "Over half of the grain raised here goes to make beer. No more market, no more money."

It took four days for the painters to paint the three rooms. When they finished, Jan inspected and approved.

"It's your house, so you have to give your approval too," she told Wayne.

It made the whole house brighter inside. Wayne could not remember when these rooms had last been painted. Now he was glad it was done.

"Cassie said she'd help you pick out some new furniture," Jan said, "and Moses, the junk-man, will take the old stuff."

Eighty-four-year-old Brigadier General Dexter L. Middleton, wearing his long johns, a battered Cavalry hat and barefoot, strode gallantly down the main Street of Marshfield waving his saber and yelling for his troops to advance on Vicksburg. The Civil War had been over for 54 years, but for the General it was 1863 and he was once again leading a charge on the left flank of the rebels dug in for a long siege.

At that time, the General had been a twenty-eight year old Colonel with the 2nd Wisconsin cavalry. Dexter was victorious in his charge and days later Vicksburg surrendered to General Grant. Dexter was promoted by Grant to Brigadier General, and it left an indelible mark on his memory.

After the war, Dexter returned to his hometown of Marshfield and was elected to the office of state Representative for the Democratic party. He retired in 1909 and lived with his youngest son Esau and his wife Marge.

In 1913, Dexter's mind began to occasionally wander, going back to Vicksburg and his great victory. As the memories became more vivid over the years, Dexter would take down his saber, which Esau had hung over the fireplace, and rally his troops for another charge, sometimes clothed, sometimes not.

The police, not trained in saber warfare, would follow the General until he ran out of steam, tell him the battle was over, and return him to his home. Finally, Esau Middleton assured the city that this action would not be repeated, as the general would be spending his remaining years at the Veterans Home in King, Wisconsin, minus the saber.

"The Marshfield brewery is closing," Helen told Billy over their morning coffee.

Billy shook his head. "That will probably put the Hempstead Barrel Company out of business too. Most of their business was with the brewery."

"It's going to put a lot of people out of work," Helen said. "I wonder how they will get by."

Wayne hummed softly to himself as he drove the county road back to town. Tomorrow, he and Cassie would pick out the new furniture for his living room. In the back of his mind was the thought 'she will live there with me soon' although neither had mentioned marriage.

Checking his gasoline gauge, Wayne decided to stop at Lemke's Standard Station for fuel. At the gas pump sat a Nash sedan, idling, with the doors open. 'Not local farmers' was the thought in Wayne's mind. He parked to the left of the front door and eased the shotgun from the rear seat. He was looking over the hood of the patrol car when two older men ran out of the station holding pistols.

"DEPUTY SHERIFF!" yelled Wayne. "Drop your weapons and get face down!"

Taken by surprise, both men stopped and stared, then opened fire!

BANG! BANG!

Wayne returned fire! *BOOM!* The shotgun blast took down the first man as a red blossom opened on his chest. The second man dropped his pistol and threw himself onto the ground.

Emil Lemke slowly opened the station door and stepped out on the small porch. Wayne handed Emil the shotgun. "Hold this while I handcuff him." The robber just stared at his dead partner as Wayne cuffed him and patted him down for any more guns.

"How much did they take?" he asked Emil.

"That man died for $14.50," Emil said. "What is this world coming to?"

"Go inside and call the sheriff's office," Wayne told him. "Tell Billy we got one for the morgue and one for the jail."

The dead man was identified by his partner as Vernon 'Vern' Frake, 39 years old, released from prison two weeks ago. The other robber was Elton Soames, 40 years old,

Vernon's cousin. This was his first journey into crime, he told Billy.

"I needed the money to buy food," he said. "Vern told me it would be easy."

"Vern lied," Billy said softly.

CHAPTER FIFTEEN

The Queen-Anne style furniture in my living room was showing its age. The divan was threadbare in spots and the seams were showing stuffing. Dad's arm chair was sagging and the footstool had a fractured foot. Wayne helped Moses Rickert load it all on his cart and gave him ten dollars to haul it away.

"Come help me arrange the chairs," yelled Cassie. In the living room sat a new sofa, a wing-back chair and a very comfortable looking easy chair Wayne was looking forward to trying out. "Your mom's rocking chair stays," she said, "it belonged to her mother and is part of your family history."

The dining room stayed the same with the oak dining table and six chairs and matching china cabinet. Dad had bought it for their 25th wedding anniversary. As he stood lost in thought, Cassie slipped her hand in his. "Let's invite my dad and mom over for dinner Friday night," she said, "you can show off the new home makeover."

'It must be near midnight' Lyle thought. He was sitting quietly in the blind facing Gandt's woods. A light breeze was keeping most of the mosquito's away. A deer had ambled by about an hour ago, just a shadow against the half-moon.

His thoughts turned to Edna. She had been dropping little hints about wanting to get married. Lyle had been giving the idea of marriage some serious thought, but not just yet. The muted crack of a stick snapped him back to reality. A slight rustle of brush made Lyle focus to his left. The form of a man showed against the moonlight, moving slowly down the game trail. The form carried no light as it rounded a bend and disappeared down the trail. About an hour later the dark form returned carrying something in its left hand. Soon it was lost in the darkness leaving behind the faint odor of mash. Lyle waited about a half-hour then left the blind, headed back to his patrol car.

The Agriculture Secretary, David Houston, addressed the crowd from a podium near the park entrance. He spoke about the new trade agreements with Europe. France, Germany and several other countries who needed the food America could provide during this time of rebuilding. Much of the farmland of France had been destroyed by trenches and artillery shells. Bodies of dead soldiers from both sides were still being found in shallow graves. It would take years for the land to recover. Meanwhile, the people must be fed. "The price of wheat and corn and dairy products will increase as the demand becomes greater," Houston explained, "and Wisconsin will help lead the world back to prosperity."

"I would like to invite you and Helen to dinner on Friday night," Wayne told Billy.

With his big toothy smile, Billy said, "I have been wondering when we would get to see the new paint job. Can we bring anything?"

"No need," Wayne said. "Cassie is taking care of everything. Lyle and Edna will also be there, and no tie, this is a casual dinner."

"Casual suits me fine," laughed Billy.

Marshfield was slowly growing out to the east and south. The mostly flat fertile farmland and the railroad were the reasons. Corn and grain mills took in the harvests and the railroad delivered the harvest to the large cities. The prices paid to farmers crept slowly upward, just enough to turn a small profit. The farm machinery business was turning out new inventions every week. A Farmall tractor pulling a four-bottom plow could do in a day what had taken a week with horses. Farmers sons saw the future, and stayed with the land. The beer state was becoming the dairy state.

Lyle was having breakfast with his father Hiram when Wayne walked into Carson's cafe.

With a warm handshake Hiram said, "Glad you made it back from the war Wayne. Terrible thing about your folks. Lost my wife, June, to that damn flu."

Taking a seat, Wayne said, "Lyle told me you are putting up a new building in Stevens Point."

"Now that the paper mill is up and running, George Meade wants a new office building," Hiram said, "have to have someplace for the big shots to hang out all day."

Later, in Billy's office, Lyle and Wayne compared notes on their nights in the blind. "They seem to work on a four hour schedule," Wayne said, "probably keeping the fire going under the cooker and adding to the mash."

"Give them a few more days." Billy said. "By then our

two Federal Revenue men should be here. They will want to catch Rodney at the still."

Carl Miller opened his market every weekday morning at 8 o'clock. He cranked the awning out to protect his vegetables from the sun, then set out the baskets. Old Eugene Everson and his wife Bernice drove up with a team of horses and wagon. The back was loaded with fresh tomatoes, corn, beans and carrots. Carl and Eugene began unloading the produce Carl would buy.

When they heard dogs barking, they looked up just in time to see the cat run under the wagon and out between the horses feet. The team bolted and took off down the street. Bernice managed to grab the reins, but the team was off and running. The cat dodged into the alley next to the furniture store, followed by the dogs, and disappeared. Hauling at the reins and yelling at the horses, Bernice managed to bring them to a stop two blocks away. Turning the horses around, she drove back to the market and the men finished unloading. The only damage was a half-dozen squashed tomatoes. The Everson's would have a fine story to tell friends.

CHAPTER SIXTEEN

The delicious aroma wafting from the kitchen made Wayne's mouth water. He was setting out the good china and silverware while Cassie, Edna, and Lyle bustled around each other in the kitchen. Jan had bought a roast, and left written instructions for Cassie to make a fine meal. Lettuce, tomatoes and onions from the garden were going into the salad Lyle was making. Edna mashed the potatoes and prepared the gravy. Cassie stirred the pot of green beans and checked the roast. A knock at the front door, and Billy called out, "Hello the house!"

Helen gasped as they entered. "It's beautiful! I love the new paint and the drapes!"

"It sure makes a big difference," Billy said.

"The roast is ready," Cassie called out.

Wayne carefully carved slices from the roast as Lyle, Cassie, and Edna set out the food. When everyone was seated, Helen said a blessing. Looking around the table, Wayne realized this was his new family.

After dinner, the men sat out on the wide front porch having coffee. Inside they could hear the women talking and laughing as the table was cleared.

"I believe Cassie is building a nest in your house," Billy said with a smile.

Blushing a little, Wayne said, "We haven't talked marriage yet." Turning to Lyle, Wayne said, "You and Edna have gotten quite close lately."

Lyle tipped his head slightly to one side. "I not only find her attractive, we seem to fit together, much like you and Cassie."

Billy sipped his coffee. "Helen and I were talking last night. It gives us both peace of mind that Cassie is happy again. The only thing missing in our lives is grandchildren."

Totally at a loss for words, Wayne just stared down at his feet. He was saved from answering when Helen, Cassie, and Edna walked out on the porch.

"Have we missed anything," Helen asked. Lyle started laughing, then Billy and Wayne.

"Just talking about the weather," Billy laughed.

Turned out that the Gandt's only had two stills, the smaller one about a half-mile behind their house, the big one in a natural hollow in the woods. Rodney was sure no one knew about the big still. The boys, Louis and Joe, took turns checking the big still every night. Rodney thought if he ever got raided by Revenue men, they would smash the small still and go away, thinking they had put him out of business. They stored the alcohol from the big still in a root cellar inside the falling-down barn.

'The time is coming when this moonshine will be worth lots of money,' thought Rodney. With prohibition starting next year, Rodney planned to haul his alcohol to Milwaukee, where an old friend had some friends in the bootleg business. For now, he and his boys would just keep making home brew.

At four in the morning the big bell at the firehouse began ringing. FIRE! Wayne rolled out of bed, slipped on his pants and opened the front door. Over toward Main Street, tongues of fire could be seen poking into the night sky. Running back to the bedroom, Wayne got dressed and then ran out to the carriage house. Backing the car around, he headed toward the fire. When a fire truck passed him, Wayne followed close behind.

The Hempstead Barrel Company was ablaze. A pumper truck was in the street and men were rolling out hoses to the fire hydrant a half-block away. Feeling a hand on his shoulder, Wayne looked around, and there was Billy.

"I've got Lyle three blocks up on Oak street detouring traffic around by Sawmill Road," he said. "You go three blocks down to Taft Ave. and do the same."

Buildings on both sides of the fire were being hosed down to keep the flames from spreading. The sound of groaning timbers and breaking glass could be heard as the old building began to cave in. All the seasoned hardwood inside used to make barrels kept the fire raging for hours. By dawn the inferno shot a fifteen-foot blaze into the morning sun.

The heat was so intense that firemen were hosing each other down to cope. When the front of the building collapsed, the flaming skeleton of a delivery truck could be seen. By nine in the morning the fire began to recede into itself. The buildings on either side were scorched, but saved. Unfortunately, the barrel company was a total loss. What remained was a pile of smoldering ash and blackened smoking posts poking through.

Hempstead and his son Theo could only watch from across the street as their business burned down. Vilas started making barrels in 1881, and, as the business grew the brewery became his main source of income. He'd retired in March, turning the business over to Theo.

"What will we do now?" Vilas kept asking, "what will we do now?"

Theo had no answer to give him.

The train made two stops in Marshfield. One at ten each morning and again at four in the afternoon. The two men who stepped down from the afternoon train looked ready to take on the toughest job. Beneath their suit coats could be seen the bulge of a pistol.

"Which way to the Sheriff's office?" one of them asked Gus Fletcher, the station-master.

"Tom can take you there in his taxi," Gus said. Tom helped them load their suitcases and drove to Billy's office.

Returning from patrol, the two deputies walked into Billy's office and saw the two hard-looking men. Standing behind his desk, Billy made the introductions. "These are my deputies, Wayne Schooley and Lyle Anderson. Boys, meet Clyde Stanley and Chester Lewis, our federal revenue agents."

Shaking hands all around, Clyde asked, "When would be the best time to catch Rodney at his cooker?"

"He's usually there by seven o'clock in the morning," Lyle said.

"We'll check in at the hotel for the night," Chester said, "and meet you back here at five tomorrow morning."

As the two men left, Lyle asked, "How do we plan to help them?"

"We take them to the blind and stand by in case they need us. They did ask me for one thing," Billy said with a smile, "I want one of you to go to the hardware store and get six sticks of dynamite."

Chester Lewis was six foot tall, with brown eyes and hair. Clyde Stanley was a bit shorter at five ten, blue eyes and blonde hair. They were waiting outside the sheriff's office when Billy arrived, and Wayne and Lyle were right behind him.

"Did you get the dynamite?" Clyde asked. Lyle held up the six sticks and a roll of fuse. Both Chester and Clyde wore a web belt with holster. In the holsters were model 1911 Colt .45's. They both carried 12 gauge pump shotguns. They all loaded into two cars and drove out of town.

Chester Lewis rode with Billy; Clyde was with Lyle and Wayne. "Where were you before this?" Wayne asked.

"Chet and I just came from Fern Hollow, Kentucky," Clyde said, "and we were glad to leave. We blew up two stills, shot two men and barely got out alive." As he talked, Clyde was cutting lengths of fuse for the dynamite, smiling all the while.

CHAPTER SEVENTEEN

Claude and his hired man were half-way through their morning milking when the patrol cars drove into his yard. Billy talked to Claude a minute then walked back to his car. "I told Claude we might make a little noise, but nothing to worry about." All but Billy got out their shotguns and loaded them with buckshot.

"While you men go have some fun, I'll go around and park in Gandt's driveway, in case he has the urge to take off," Billy said. As Billy left, the four armed officers headed down the trail to the blind.

It was just light enough to walk without the aid of a lantern. When they reached the blind, Clyde pulled a pocket watch from his pants, checked the time and said, "five minutes after six. Let's all be real quiet."

A few squirrels moved around and an owl winged silently overhead. The scrape of wood against metal alerted them to someone coming. It was Rodney and Louis. Rodney carried a shotgun, Louis carried a covered bucket. They passed out of sight around the long bend, Rodney talking, Louis nodding his head.

Just above a whisper, Chester said, "We'll give them a half hour to get set up, then Clyde and I will follow. You two stay and block the trail in case one gets by us."

Checking his watch again, Clyde smiled. "Hey Chet, this reminds me of about a year ago in Tennessee, remember?"

Chester grinned and replied "I remember that moonshiner that tried to take your head off with an axe."

"He would have," Clyde said, "but you shot the axe out of his hands."

"Lucky for you," said Chet, "I was aiming for his head."

Wayne and Lyle glanced at each other, not knowing what to believe.

Clyde and Chester slipped quietly down the trail, following the sounds coming from the still. The smell of cooking mash got stronger as the two men came up to a large hollow. Louis was stirring the mash as Rodney held a jug under the spigot.

"FEDERAL REVENUE AGENTS!" Clyde shouted. "Get down on the ground now!" Louis looked around, saw the two men with shotguns, and flopped down on the ground. Rodney dropped his jug and took off through the brush, with Clyde in hot pursuit. Rodney was in no shape to run far and Clyde barreled into him, knocking him flat.

"Get on your feet with your hands in the air," Clyde ordered.

With Rodney and Louis tied to a tree, Chester placed four sticks of dynamite around the still. The fuses were different lengths, allowing the men time to get clear and make sure all four went off. There were tears in Rodney's eyes as he watched Chester, but he never said a word.

"Take those two up the trail," Chester said, 'I'll light these fuses and be right behind you." Clyde untied Louis and Rodney but kept their hands tied. As they slowly walked away, the first stick blew.

BOOM!

Rodney staggered to his knees, openly crying. Louis just stood with his mouth wide open.

BOOM!

"Keep moving." Clyde poked Rodney with his shotgun.

BOOM!

BOOM!

Wayne and Lyle came flying down the trail, hoping everyone was alive just as Chester appeared with a big smile on his face. "I guess I've still got the touch."

Wanting to see for themselves, Wayne and Lyle went to look at what had been the still. Torn and twisted pieces of metal lay all around. The smell of hot mash hung in the air like a cloud. Reaching down, Lyle picked up a foot long piece of coil. With a smile he said, "A souvenir for Billy."

Claude was waiting for them as the group got back to the patrol car. "I heard the explosions, all four of them. That must have been a sight," he said.

Billy drove in and was laughing as he got out of the car.

"You got all but one," he said, "Joe must have run and hid when he heard that dynamite go off."

Lyle handed Billy the piece of coil from the still. "Something to hang on your wall," he said with a grin.

"Let's take them back to town and put them in jail where they belong," Clyde said, "then me and Chet have some business to take care of in West Virginia."

Joe had been sleeping when the first charge of dynamite went off. Rolling out of bed, he looked out the kitchen window and saw Billy's car in the driveway. The second charge went off, and Joe got dressed in a hurry. When the third stick blew Joe was already running out the back door carrying a shotgun. When the final stick of dynamite exploded, Joe knew his dad and Louis would not be home anytime soon. He hid out the rest of the day at the small still, wondering what to do next. He was on his own, at least for now, and he intended to stay that way as long as he could. In a few days he would go into Marshfield and see if Louis and his dad were in jail. 'Dad will tell me what to do' he thought, 'till then, I guess I'll keep the small still going.'

Rodney didn't start talking until the cell door slammed shut, then he wouldn't shut up. He cursed the men who put him in jail, the town and the people in it, law enforcement in general and the government as a whole. Louis just sat on his bunk and stared at the floor. The jailer brought them trays of food at sundown—beef stew, cornbread and coffee. Later that night, they huddled together.

"What do we do now?" Louis asked.

"Joe will be here in a day or so," whispered Rodney, "I'll have him get us a lawyer so we can get out of here."

"Lawyers cost money," Louis whined, "and you don't have any."

CHAPTER EIGHTEEN

"I'm going to let Louis go," Billy said.

Wayne asked "Why?" Wayne asked, puzzled.

Leaning back in his chair, Billy explained. "We blew up the still, but where is all that alcohol he has been making? Louis is going to lead us right to it."

"What about Joe?" Lyle asked.

"Joe is a little smarter than Louis," Billy said, "he won't go near that hidden booze until Rodney says so. Louis, on the other hand, will take us right to it."

Billy opened the cell door. "Come on out Louis, I'm letting you go. It was Rodney's still, not yours. You just happened to be there. I got no cause to hold you." Bewildered, Louis looked to Rodney for guidance.

Rodney shrugged his shoulders and said, "Go take care of your brother."

Louis walked out of the jail and slowly started the long walk home.

The fairgrounds in Marshfield was getting a facelift. Several buildings were torn down and rebuilt. The bleachers were gone over with a magnifying glass. Last year, nine-year-old Jimmy Schaefer had jumped up and down on a board until it broke and he fell through. A few scratches on his leg sent his mother Glenda into a screaming fit, not at her son but at the county for being negligent on repairs.

The stock barns were repainted and some new lights were added for the annual baseball game. Hitching rails were removed to provide more parking for autos. The Blue Sky Fireworks Company had applied for a permit to hold a display on the last day of the fair. It would be a grand affair, as usual.

Wayne was heading back into town about five in the afternoon when the ambulance passed him, going the other way, at a high rate of speed. Turning around, he followed. Three miles later the ambulance turned down a dirt road and a mile later drove into Walter Yeske's hayfield with Wayne right behind him. The Farmall tractor with a half-full wagon and a hayloader behind sat there. A man was on the ground and another man was beside him.

"What happened?" Wayne asked as he approached. It was Walter's son, Andrew, on the ground. Next to him was his father. Andrew was in pain but laughing.

"It was the darndest thing you ever saw," he said, "the hay-loader picked up a big snake and dumped it on my neck. I dropped the pitchfork and grabbed the snake to throw it off me. I turned around, tripped over the pitchfork and fell off the front of the wagon." Andrew winced as he touched his left leg below the knee. "One wheel rolled over my leg. I think it broke."

The doctor who had been examining Andrew's leg nodded his head. "It's broke." The wagon was an older one with steel wheels, heavy enough empty, this one had a half load of hay.

A Model T pickup truck drove up. Andrew's mother, Freda, had called the hospital and returned. With Wayne's help Andrew was loaded into the ambulance. "Freda, you go with him. I got to get this load of hay in."

Looking across the field, Wayne saw it was half cleared. Taking off his uniform shirt, he tossed it in his patrol car and climbed up on the wagon.

"Let's go Walter," he said, "we can finish this load, take it to the barn, then I'll give you a ride into St. Joseph's."

"By golly son, you got a deal," Walter said with a big grin. "Billy picked a winner when he hired you!"

It was almost dark when Wayne got home. Jan was in the kitchen stirring something in a pot. "The whole town is talking about Andy Yeske and you," she said.

"And what are they saying?" Wayne asked.

Jan laughed. "They're calling Andy the snake wrestler and you're now the hay making Deputy!"

"What is that delicious smell coming from that pan?" asked Wayne.

Jan set the pot on the table. "Chicken and dumplings. Thought you might be hungry after playing farmer all afternoon."

Louis and Joe decided to just keep the small still going until they heard from Rodney. Joe had been on his way into town when he picked up Louis halfway home.

"Tomorrow we get dad a lawyer and let them decide what to do," Joe said.

"Lawyers cost money, and Dad doesn't have any," Louis repeated.

"Yes he does," Joe told him. There is a coffee can of money stashed in the root cellar with the whiskey. Dad never told you about it because he knew you would take it. There should be enough for a lawyer."

"We don't know any lawyers," Louis said, "how do we find one?"

Thinking a minute, Joe said, "About twice a month, there's a guy who buys a quart of whiskey from Dad. I remember Dad saying he was a lawyer named McGruder from Spencer. We'll go see him."

After supper, Wayne took a walk over to the Anderson's. Cassie sat in the porch swing reading the paper.

"Any good news?" Wayne called as he walked up the porch steps.

"There's my haymaker," Cassie said with a giggle. "Walter Yeske told me all about it."

"How is Andrew?"

"He's fine. Just worried how Walter will run the farm without him."

Billy walked out on the porch and smiled at Wayne. "You did just what I would have done, and tomorrow Lyle said he would take a turn on the hay wagon with Walter. Makes me proud of both of you."

Cassie reached out her hand. "Sit with me on the swing a while, Wayne."

"I'll leave you two alone," Billy said and went back in the house.

"Now we can kiss and hold hands," Cassie whispered. Even the mosquito's moved away, giving the lovers their privacy.

CHAPTER NINETEEN

Cecil McGruder scratched the widening bald spot on top of his graying hair. At 63, he struggled to maintain his law practice. He was just an inch under six foot, gaunt, barely weighed 140 lbs., and his knees hurt, constantly. His small office in Spencer was next to the pharmacy on Casper street. His business lately consisted mostly of drafting wills, some real estate work and the occasional property dispute.

When Joe and Louis walked into his office he knew immediately who they were and why they were there. He'd followed the story in the Marshfield news, wondering if he'd still be able to buy the homemade whiskey that seemed to help the pain in his knees. Standing behind his desk, he held out his hand. "Good day gentlemen" he said, "how may I help you?"

"Dad's in jail and needs a lawyer," said Joe. "How much would you charge to help him?"

Thinking quickly, which seldom happened with Cecil, he said, "I would need a $50 retainer. Then I'll go talk to Rodney and see what can be done." Joe handed Cecil two twenties and a ten.

"I need a receipt to show Dad," he said.

"I will talk to him this afternoon," said Cecil with a smile as he handed them a receipt.

Rodney was not overly excited to see Cecil. He knew he needed some legal advice but was concerned about Cecil's ability to deliver it.

"When they destroyed your still, did they find any whiskey?" Cecil asked.

"No they didn't," Rodney answered. "I keep the whiskey hid somewhere else."

"Without any whiskey as evidence, we may be able to convince the judge that you never actually produced any alcohol," Cecil explained, "but only attempted to."

"Do you really think a judge will believe that?" Rodney asked.

"It doesn't matter. You need a defense, and this may be the only one you have."

Thinking hard, which gave Rodney a headache, he said, "I'll probably still get some jail time, won't I?"

"It's entirely possible," said Cecil, "but it will be less than you would get with no attorney."

"How much are you charging me for this?" Rodney asked.

"Your son already gave me $50. Another $150 will cover all legal expenses," Cecil explained. Knowing he had little choice, Rodney nodded his head in acceptance.

Walter and Freda Yeske were hosting a Sunday afternoon cookout for Billy and Helen, Wayne and Cassie and Lyle and Edna. The hay was in the barn and Andrew was hobbling around on crutches. It was 90 degrees and humid, but there was a light southerly breeze making it seem cooler. The big shaded front porch was alive with chatter and laughter. In the yard, bratwurst slowly cooked to perfection on the grill.

From the kitchen came the sounds of women laying out salads, pickles, catsup, rolls and dinnerware. Cold beer and iced tea were served and drank. It was a family thanking another family for helping out in a time of need. No gushing 'thank you' was given because none was needed. You helped those in need because you might be the next one in need. Farm families knew this more than any other. It was the lifeline that held a community together.

Andrew had invited his girlfriend, Lucy Granger, a neighbors daughter. Shy at first, she soon felt comfortable with Cassie and Edna. Freda Yeske was enjoying having her kitchen filled with females. Sometimes she went weeks without another woman's presence in the house. She hoped Andrew and Lucy would soon marry and give her grandchildren. The house was plenty big enough for another family.

"Bring me a pan Freda," yelled Walter from the yard. "These bratwurst are ready to eat!"

It was Monday afternoon when Edna Weber realized she was finally and totally in love with Lyle Peterson. The picnic at the Yeske farm had been one of the best days of her young life. She constantly thought about Lyle, how he looked at her and treated her. She had been dating since she was sixteen, her looks and personality had drawn the young men to her from all around the county. She could have had her pick of several eligible suitors, but none had captured her heart like

Lyle. It had not happened when they first met, or even after their first date. But by the second date there was something about Lyle that made her heart beat a little faster. Blushing, she caught herself wondering if their children would look like him.

Lyle was a little shy, which made him more attractive. Her mother noticed and silently approved. Her father, Daryl, knew something was happening, but wasn't sure what.

"That's two orders you got wrong today," he said, "do you feel alright?" Smiling,

Edna patted his shoulder. "Everything is fine, Dad," she said. "Just thinking about Lyle."

"Are you two getting serious about each other?" Daryl asked.

Laughing, Edna smiled. "I love him dad, and I know he loves me. Right now, that is the most wonderful feeling in the world."

Slowly shaking his head, Daryl muttered, "just keep your mind on your work."

"So that's where Rodney's been hiding his whiskey," Billy whispered. He'd been watching the Gandt place through his Army surplus binoculars. About noon , Billy had parked a mile up the road from the Gandt's driveway and walked down to a spot in the field about 150 yards from their house.

The dilapidated old barn sat off to one side of the house. It leaned toward the rear and half the roof was gone. Joe had entered once, carrying a jug. He came out later without the jug. Louis entered the barn carrying nothing and came out later with a jug.

'Must be a cellar in there,' thought Billy. Walking back to his patrol car, Billy began planning a way to get his hands on that cache of booze. He still had two sticks of dynamite left from the first raid that he hoped to use.

CHAPTER TWENTY

"I won't be here for supper tonight mom," Cassie said as she walked in the front door. Still in her nurses uniform, she went to her room to change.

"When is Wayne coming to pick you up?" Helen called.

"In about an hour. We're going to the movie with Lyle and Edna, then to Carson's Cafe to eat."

"Lyle and Edna seem to be very close lately," remarked Helen when Cassie returned.

"I think Lyle is going to ask Edna to marry him," Cassie said with a smile, "and I know Edna will say yes."

Laying her hand gently on Cassie's arm, Helen asked, "Have you and Wayne made any plans yet?"

Cassie gave her mother a hug. "We love each other, and for now that is enough."

The movie was *Wagon Tracks* starring William S. Hart, a western with a romantic plot. Collette Neuman followed the action on the screen, playing the piano, fast and loud during the gun fights and soft and slow in the in the love scenes. All too soon, the film ended and the lights came on.

"I'd someday like to see how one of these movies is made," Cassie said, "it's remarkable how they film all that action."

"I think the camera is mounted on a truck," Lyle said.

"What amazes me," added Wayne, " is the horses don't get spooked by the gunfire."

"They do have some good kissing scenes," Edna said with a giggle.

The next morning before they left on patrol, Billy called Wayne and Lyle into the office. "Rodney has been hiding his whiskey in that tumble-down barn. There must be a cellar in there."

"Will a judge let us look to make sure?" Wayne asked.

"If my plan works, we won't need a Judge." Billy grinned.

August has always been an unpredictable month in Wisconsin. A seemingly cloudless morning can turn into a rainstorm by afternoon. Wayne had been feeling a change in the weather just in the past hour. The wind was picking up, coming from the southwest. Dark clouds rolled in followed by lightning and thunder. Fat raindrops began pockmarking the dry earth. Then the rain came fast and heavy.

CRACK! BOOM! Constant lightning and thunder. Wayne was parked in the driveway of an old abandoned farm, the rain so heavy he couldn't see the front of his patrol car. The hail started small, then grew in size, as big as golf balls! It lasted nearly five minutes, then tapered off and finally stopped. The rain continued for another half hour then it too stopped. Within minutes, the wind died down, the sky cleared and the sun came out, like nothing at all had happened.

Driving into town, Wayne surveyed the damage from the hail. Fields of corn were beaten down, barn roofs were missing shingles and some had holes. In the town itself, stores had broken windows, awnings were in tatters and tree branches littered the streets. Every auto, including his patrol car, had dents, some with broken windows.

Two men carrying an older woman came out of the flower shop. Wayne stopped, got out and opened his rear door.

"Put her in my car," he directed, "I'll take her to St Josephs." The two older men, placed the woman in the car and then got in with her. One man held a bloody towel to her head.

"What happened?" asked Wayne. "She went out to cover the flowers, and got hit in the head with hail," said one of the men.

"I never in my life seen hail that big," said the other man. After dropping them aff at the hospital, Wayne went back to help where he could.

The wind, rain and hail had been just too much for the old barn at the Gandt place. It resembled a large old animal on its last legs. It sagged to the left, slowly twisted to the right, bowed to the front and with a death-like groan settled to the ground. Watching from the safety of the house, Joe hung his head.

After the storm he and Louis began tearing apart the roof, uncovering the timbers that covered the cellar. It took four hours to move enough old lumber to be able to open the cellar door. Then, they removed all the whiskey, 175 tightly-sealed one-quart jars, and stored them in an empty bedroom in the house. Joe put a lock on the door to keep Louis from helping himself to a quart now and then. Then he drove the old truck into Marshfield to give Rodney the bad news.

Cecil Mcgruder pecked away at his old Underwood typewriter. It had cost him $75 new in 1896, when he had an actual law practice. It missed a letter now and then and the keys sometimes stuck, but Cecil labored on. Drafting a defense for Rodney meant stretching and bending the truth until it was unrecognizable, but, as the old saying went, 'Work with what you have, not what you wish you had.'

The judge hearing the case was the Honorable Willard Tatum, a cranky old curmudgeon with little tolerance for criminals. Reaching into the bottom drawer of his file cabinet, Cecil lifted out a half-full quart jar of home brew and took a drink. His knees hurt, and the whiskey seemed to help. Rolling the paper from the typewriter, Cecil placed it in the file folder on his desk. It was time to visit his client, Rodney Gandt in Marshfield.

Jan Magnuson was canning vegetables. Today it was green beans and yellow wax beans. She had found four cases of quart canning jars in the cellar that had never been opened. Another smaller box held new lids and cakes of wax. Bringing it all up into the kitchen, she took out the almost new pressure-cooker that Wayne's mother had purchased the year before.

The beans were plentiful this summer, and Jan picked and washed two baskets. Snipping the ends and cutting them for canning was therapy for her; it gave her a sense of the family she'd always enjoyed.

It was late afternoon when Cassie arrived. "How many quarts today?" she asked with a smile.

"Eight quarts," Jan answered. "Four green and four yellow."

Did you plant your own garden this year?"

Jan smiled. "Wayne and I agreed that his garden plot was big enough to hold what I would have planted at home. This way, I only have one garden to care for."

"You like working for Wayne, don't you?" Cassie stated.

"Yes I do! He is a fine young man, and I will take care of his house until you are ready to take over."

Giggling and blushing at the same time, Cassie said, "Oh Jan, we haven't made any plans yet."

Jan patted Cassie's hand softly. "A blind man could see you two are in love and a perfect match."

Rodney took the news about the barn better than Joe had expected. He rolled his eyes then slowly shook his head. "After the hearing, I'll decide what to do. Until then, keep Louis from drinking it all up."

"I put a lock on the door and nailed the window shut," Joe told him. "He's tending the small still now."

"McGruder is coming this afternoon with some papers to sign. Old Tatum is the Judge, and he won't go easy on me." The father and son sat quietly for a time, then Joe left.

Lyle had made up his mind. He was going to trade in his beloved Indian motorcycle for an automobile. He had purchased the bike from a friend who's young wife was pregnant and they needed family transportation. But, now, it was Lyle's turn to decide where his life was headed.

He'd made up his mind to ask Edna to marry him. He loved her and wanted to be a responsible husband and father. Edna loved riding in the sidecar, the wind blowing through her dark hair. Yet, Lyle was torn between the freedom of the motorcycle and the anticipation of Edna as his wife. Maybe next week he'd start looking for a car.

The day started hot and humid, which meant the courtroom would be the same. Willard Tatum had been an attorney for 22 years and a judge for 35 years. Lately, his arthritis had settled in his lower back and days like this made him irritable. The special cushion for his courtroom chair helped, but any movement was painful. He walked with a cane now, moving slower than usual to maintain his balance. He did not drive an auto. Instead, his seventeen-year-old grandson, Avery, was his driver.

At the courthouse, Avery helped him out of the 1917 four-door Nash touring car. "Be back here at five o'clock," Willard said, "and this time, be on time."

There were four cases on the docket today. A burglary, a drunk and disorderly, an auto theft and the moonshiner, Rodney Gandt. Taking two pills for pain, the judge was ready.

CHAPTER TWENTY-ONE

Joe and Louis arrived at the jail early. They brought Rodney's old gray suit and a white shirt. A shoebox containing shaving gear was inspected by the jailer then given to Rodney. While Rodney was shaving, Cecil McGruder arrived, clean-shaven and wearing a black suit and tie. "Ours is the last case to be heard" Cecil said, "I expect it to be called after lunch."

"It was about two years ago that Dad was in court for being drunk in public," Joe remembered, "and Judge Tatum gave him 30 days."

"The Judge will also remember," said Cecil, "he may be old, but his memory is as sharp as ever."

In his chambers Judge Tatum was having his morning coffee and reviewing the Gandt case. Sheriff Anderson had covered it well. When he read the report about the federal Agents dynamiting the still he laughed aloud. This was the kind of law enforcement he approved of. 'Takes me back to my younger days,' thought the Judge.

Years ago, before the courthouse was built, court was held in saloons, churches and once in the parlor of a whore house before the locals burned it down. He recalled a fist fight with a lawyer from Illinois who didn't know when to shut up. The judge won by breaking the lawyer's nose. Some men had been released, some jailed and a few hung.

The bailiff brought him back to the present, knocking on his door and announcing "It's time your honor." Finishing his coffee and gathering his papers, the Judge Tatum made his way slowly into the courtroom.

Sheriff Billy decided only one deputy was needed to testify. Wayne would be on patrol while he and Lyle were in court. The bailiff had told him the case would come up after lunch, so no need to hurry. Billy's plan to blow up Gandt's old barn to get at the whiskey had fallen through when the barn collapsed. He was sure the home brew was now in the house, but he needed proof. Even though Wayne and Lyle were doing regular patrols past the Gandt's home, they had seen nothing. 'Patience' thought Billy, 'patience.'

The thermometer outside the courthouse read 94 degrees by lunch time. Everything was still without a hint of a breeze to stir the leaves on the oak trees in the park. Dust from passing cars left a brown haze that hung in the humid air. Everyone and everything moved in slow motion; even the flies entering the open courthouse windows barely moving their wings.

"All rise," called the bailiff as Judge Tatum entered from his chambers. Settling gingerly into his chair, the judge nodded at the bailiff.

"Case number 5165, operating an illegal whiskey still," intoned the bailiff.

"Hello again, Mr. Gandt," the judge said. "You are charged with the operation of a whiskey still. How do you plead?"

Cecil stood slowly, his knees aching. "My client wishes to plead guilty with extenuating circumstance your Honor."

"And what circumstance would that be?" Judge Tatum looked up from the court file.

"Although Mr. Gandt did build and operate a still, it was destroyed before any whiskey was produced," answered Cecil.

Turning his gaze to the sheriff, Judge Tatum asked, "was there any whiskey found at the still?"

Billy stood. There was a small amount that was destroyed when the still was blown up, judge."

Turning back to Cecil, the judge said, "The fact that no whiskey was found has no bearing on this case. The still was illegal and Mr. Gandt was operating it. Have your client stand for sentencing." Rodney stood, his eyes staring down at the floor. "Mr. Rodney Gandt, this court sentences you to a term of no less than six months and no more than one year in the county jail. Court is dismissed."

Back in his jail cell, Rodney, Louis and Joe huddled together. "For now, the whiskey stays where it is" Rodney told his sons. "In about a month, when things quiet down, I'll decide our next move. Until then make as much whiskey as you can from the small still." Turning to Louis, Rodney said, "Lay off drinking up the profits and take orders from Joe."

The boys left, taking the suit with them. Cecil McGruder had left right after court and Rodney hoped he'd seen the last of him.

The August board meeting of the Doctors at St. Joseph's Hospital was underway. Six pitchers of ice water sat on large coasters atop the mahogany table. Coats and ties had been dispensed with and handheld fans waved vigorously. The mood was optimistic. No new cases of the Spanish flu had been reported for the first two weeks of the month. A total of 943 cases had been treated since the start of the flu, with only three recoveries, all children under the age of twelve.

The staff of the hospital had been hit hard. Four doctors and seven nurses had died. Cardinal Lewelyn had been often quoted saying, 'The angel of death plays no favorites.' The only treatments used to combat the flu were gargling with saltwater, daily doses of aspirin for pain and lots of fresh air. By July of 1919, the flu seemed to have run its course. By August, only a few mild cases were reported with no deaths.

Joe and Louis cut firewood to feed the fire that cooked the mash. Louis sawed the logs into chunks while Joe split the chunks into smaller pieces. It seemed to Louis that it took forever to get any whiskey from the small still. A slow, steady drip took about three hours to fill a quart jar. By late afternoon, three jars had been filled. Joe would add these to the stockpile in the house. The goal was two hundred quarts of home brew. The total now was 177. Only 23 quarts to go.

CHAPTER TWENTY-TWO

It began as just a dark cloud moving in from the west. Then the hot breeze grew stronger and became a wind. The dark cloud grew a pigtail which gyrated in the air and pointed toward earth. The pigtail grew longer and thicker, becoming a black snake still trying to touch the ground. Turning and twisting, the tail of the black snake briefly kissed the ground, then lifted to savor the taste of the gritty dirt.

The snake was now a funnel, and the hot wind drove it back to earth. It dug its way into the farmland, throwing clods of grass and dirt into the howling wind. The funnel spread wider, bending, breaking and uprooting trees . A farmhouse, barn and machine shed stood in its way, and were consumed by the tornado.

The barn disappeared within the funnel, and was spewed out as broken beams and splintered boards. The house rose into the air, then was tossed aside , a pile of rubble. The funnel rose briefly at times, skipping across low areas and then dropped back down to ravage whatever was in its path. Then, like a spoiled child having tired of its anger, the funnel slowly lifted from earth, receding back into the dark cloud from which it came.

The tornado had touched down about five miles east of Marshfield. It wreaked havoc for almost a mile, destroying the Schumacher farm before it lifted back into the clouds. Daniel and Virginia Schumacher were not home at the time, a trip to the feed store for salt blocks had probably saved their lives. Wayne was on patrol and followed the path of the tornado from a safe distance. The livestock and horses had scattered, and most had survived. As he slowly drove up to what had been the Schumacher farm, Wayne stared open-mouthed at the damage. The barn was gone, but the silo next to it was untouched. The house had been lifted from its foundation and dumped fifty yards out into a cornfield. The machine shed had the roof torn off, but the Farmall tractor had not been moved.

A model-T Ford pickup truck turned off the town road and drove up to Wayne's car. It was the Schumacher's, back from the feed store. "Oh, my god!" yelled Virginia, and she began crying.

"My farm is gone," whispered Daniel as he stared at the ruins around him.

"Oh Dan," cried Virginia, "What will we do now?"

"Do you have insurance" Wayne asked.

"Yes we do," Daniel said, "but all that paperwork was in the house!"

"Your agent will have copies of everything," Wayne told them, "go see him now. Bring him out here to see the damage and take pictures with his camera."

Later, Wayne handed Billy his report on the tornado, saying "I haven't seen anything like it since the shelling during the war."

Lyle arrived with his report. "People are already talking about a barn raising for Dan and Ginnie."

"If I recall," Billy said, "Dan is a cousin to your father, Hiram, am I right Lyle?"

Lyle nodded. "Their son Jacob was killed in the war."

"Well, whatever this office can do to help, we will," Billy stated.

Leaving the office, Wayne asked Lyle, "Do Dan and Virginia have a place to live for now?"

Smiling, Lyle said, "Until plans are made, they will stay with me. And Dad is coming home to start building them a new house."

Cassie was in the kitchen with Jan when Wayne got home. He told them about the tornado taking the Schumacher farm. "What about all his cows and his team of horses," asked Cassie.

"The neighbors will round up the cattle and horses," Wayne said, "and they will take care of them until a new barn is built."

"At every barn raising, the men will need to be fed," Jan said, "and I will be there to help."

Joe and Louis Gandt had taken shelter in the basement of their house. When all was quiet they stepped outside. The tornado had passed them by, skipping over them like a flat stone thrown on the water. At the still, the slow but steady drip of the whiskey was reassuring. "That's three more quarts today," Joe said. "Only twenty to go."

The Marshfield News devoted three pages to the damage done by the tornado, with pictures of the devastation to the Schumacher farm. A local fund was started to help rebuild the house and barn. Every business in Marshfield had some type of container on their counter with a sign stating: 'Schumacher farm.' Lumber was donated from as far away as Medford and offers of help poured in. Hiram Peterson made his living as a carpenter, and began organizing people and a plan to rebuild.

"Now Ginnie can have the bigger kitchen she wanted," Dan said with a smile. Every day Dan carefully dug through the ruins of the old house. Much had been destroyed, but there were a few surprises. A tea set given to Virginia as a wedding gift by her grandmother consisted of six cups and saucers and a teapot. All the cups and saucers were broken, but the teapot was found intact without a chip or crack. Dan's twelve gauge shotgun was found under the parlor rug, and pictures from their wedding and of their son Jacob in his uniform were salvaged—remnants of the past that could not be replaced with something new, priceless treasures to passed down to another generation.

Hiram Peterson and the insurance agent, Lester Wilburn, were trying to set the exact amount of the payment for the Schumachers.

"Dammit, Lester, they lost everything," Hiram argued, "now it's time for your company to step up and do the right thing."

Wiping his sweaty brow with a soggy handkerchief, Lester hollered, "Hiram, I can add another $500 for hardwood floors, but that is the best I can do."

"The crew I hired start Monday," Hiram said. "I'm working for nothing but the crew has to be paid. When can you get Dan and Ginnie a check?"

Letting out a sigh, Lester said, "I'll push this through and have a check for them by Wednesday."

The donated lumber and roofing would help to offset what the insurance didn't cover. The paper-mill baron, George Meade, had read the story in the newspaper. One of his staff told him the Schumachers were relatives of his favorite carpenter, Hiram Peterson. Mr. Meade wrote out a personal check for $1500 to Daniel and Virginia, with a note saying, "I hope this helps. Hiram is a valued employee who will do an excellent job."

Wayne and Lyle continued their regular patrols. Whenever possible they checked on the Gandt brothers. An occasional trip into town to visit their father seemed to be the only activity.

Rodney needed something to occupy his free time. "I'll get you some paint and a brush," Billy suggested, "and you can paint your cell."

Out of boredom, Rodney agreed. It took him a week, and the dingy brown was covered by a pale green, two coats. His spirits lifted, and he offered to paint the other two cells as well.

"You know. People pay good money to have their houses painted," Billy said. "You could start your own business and put your boys to work."

'Maybe I will' thought Rodney, 'just maybe.'

CHAPTER TWENTY-THREE

On the first day of August, 1919, the Marshfield Rotary Club no. 522 was granted its charter. Active members were Alois Firnstahl, John Upham II, Elizabeth Schmall and Henry Purdy. All of them had lost family members in the Great War. Being members of the business community, they were active in other clubs, had promoted the War Bond drives, raised money for the new grade school and helped to establish the Fire Department.

In establishing the Rotary Club, these four people had a specific goal in mind. Their first order of business was to finance and erect a memorial in the park dedicated to the brave men who had given their lives in the war. Many American soldiers bodies were never returned to their families for burial in a home cemetery. Their remains were interred in a field in France under a cross bearing the name of the deceased . The Rotary Club would have their names and military rank inscribed in stone. A tribute to their fathers, brothers and sons who perished. Their sacrifice would never be forgotten.

The time had come. Lyle Peterson borrowed Wayne's Studebaker. "You must have something special in mind," Wayne said smiling.

Lyle grinned. "My plans tonight do not include a motorcycle." Lyle picked up Edna from the diner as she got off of work.

"Where are we going?" she asked as she slid into the passenger seat.

"I found the perfect spot on the bank of the Eau Pliene river and we're going to watch a magnificent sunset."

As they drove, Edna asked "How's the new house coming along at the Schumacher farm?"

"Dad and his crew have it framed up," Lyle said. "Now they're running pipe so Ginnie will have a hand pump in the kitchen." They reached the spot on the riverbank just as the sun began its descent. The molten red-gold orb was surrounded by a shimmering background of orange, violet, soft yellow and blazing red.

"Oh Lyle, it's beautiful!" sighed Edna. With trembling fingers, Lye reached into his shirt pocket and withdrew a small box. Edna's eyes grew wide as she saw it. From the box Lyle took out a silver ring and held it out to her. "I love you Edna Weber. Will you marry me?"

Edna's hands were covering her mouth to keep from screaming. With tears dripping down her eyes, she whispered, "Oh yes, Oh my God, Yes! I love you so much Lyle. This is what I have been wishing for."

Lyle slipped the engagement ring on her finger, took her lovely face in his hands and kissed her. When the sun finally slid from the sky, the young lovers never even noticed it was gone.

At her parents' house later, Edna proudly displayed her new ring. Her mother Patti hugged them both, shedding a few tears in happiness. Daryl went to the kitchen pantry and returned with a small bottle of cherry brandy and four small glasses.

"My daughter has shown excellent taste in men, just as her mother did," he said laughing.

Mother and daughter quickly began making plans for a wedding. "When do you plan the ceremony?" Patti asked. The rest of the evening was spent picking and discarding dates for the wedding. It was decided the wedding would be late next spring on a Saturday with a small reception at the church. Lyle, still in a semi-daze, was agreeable to almost every plan.

Daryl smiled to himself, remembering his own engagement to Patti. "Lyle, let's go out on the porch and let the women have their cry, which I know from experience is coming, again."

As they sat in the twilight breeze, Daryl said, "Patti and I allowed Edna to begin dating when she was sixteen. It seemed every week or two a new young man would show up, then be gone. Edna was looking for just the right man, and I'm pleased it was you."

Lyle was glad that Daryl could not see his blush. He could hear Edna and Patti laughing and talking inside. He was no longer nervous, but his chest felt too small to hold his heart.

It was Saturday morning, and the barn raising at the Schumacher farm was underway. Newspaper reporters from all across the state interviewed anyone who was standing still. Cameras documented the event. Two state congressmen appeared briefly to give their opinions, although neither had ever held a hammer or saw. Farmers, store owners, two off-duty policemen, volunteer firemen, rail-yard workers and it seemed every man who had ever held a carpenter tool showed up.

The frame was up and in place as the trusses were set. Hiram directed the work, sorting out the carpenters and general laborers and matching them into workable groups. As the roof was being laid, the door fitted and the windows set in place, men began sorting the siding boards. Kegs of nails were opened and emptied. Older men and young boys picked up the scrap ends and stacked them in a pile to be used as firewood later.

Virginia, Jan and at least a dozen other women were getting the noon food ready. A fifty-five gallon oil drum had been cut in half, fitted with grills and laid with charcoal to cook the food. Plank tables on saw horses bearing all manner and color of tablecloths were made ready. Stacks of plates and silverware along with cups and glasses appeared from baskets. Sliced loaves of home baked bread and pitchers of iced tea and milk would grace the plank tables.

"Oh, it's lovely!"

"Congratulations!" Edna was showing off her new engagement ring. Wayne and Cassie were the first to see it that morning.

"So that's why you borrowed the car," Wayne said as he shook Lyle's hand.

"I was afraid that if Edna got too excited, she would tip

the cycle over," Lyle said, laughing. Then, he gripped Wayne's shoulder. "I'd really like you to be my best man, after all, you're my best friend."

"I will gladly, and when I ask Cassie to marry me, you must return the favor."

"When do you plan to ask her?"

"When the time is right," Wayne said, glancing toward Cassie.

By sundown the barn was up and the men stood back looking upon the structure with pride. The inside still needed work. The stanchions would arrive in the next day or so, the electric and water would be added and the floor for the haymow would need to be hammered in. The roofers would lay down the rolls of tar paper and shingles tomorrow. Dan and Virginia Schumacher stood in the drive, arms around each other, staring at the structure.

"It's bigger and better than the old one," Dan said.

"Lines of worry creased Virginia's brow. "All the hay we cut for the winter is gone," she said, "and even if we do a third cutting, there won't be enough."

Dan smiled and patted her shoulder. "Silas Brandt, Harlan Keyes and Chester Nielsen all told me they are bringing their third cut of hay to fill the mow."

Turning slowly, they looked at the half-complete new house. "Hiram has done a wonderful job on the barn and house," Virginia said.' "How will we ever repay him, Dan?"

"If we offered him money he'd refuse. As cousins, we spent a lot of our boyhood together and then lost touch as we grew. We will find a way to show our thanks."

CHAPTER TWENTY-FOUR

Edna's engagement ring was the culprit. Since Cassie had returned to Marshfield, she and Wayne had reached an understanding. They loved each other and someday would be man and wife. They were not in any hurry to rush into marriage, but Cassie did want some kind of commitment from Wayne. When they talked of the future they'd always avoided any mention of wedlock, but now Lyle and Edna were engaged!

'Why don't I at least have a locket, or maybe even a ring to show that I am promised to him?' Cassie thought. She silently vowed to tell Wayne how she felt.

Wayne had similar thoughts, but a secret fear held his tongue. He had beaten the angel of death once and it had left a scar. Now he was a lawman, a deputy with a badge who never knew if the day would end with a gunshot. Cassie had been engaged to a doctor who was killed in the war. If they got engaged and he was killed in a gunfight, could she ever move forward with her life?

Their conversations lately had been like two people crossing a flowing stream by stepping from rock to rock, moving forward without touching the water. 'The only way to find out is to ask Cassie straight out,' thought Wayne. In his dresser drawer were his parents wedding and engagement rings. Maybe it was time to step *into* the water and *carry* his love across the stream.

In all his seventeen years, Arlen Mayhew had never expected to have this much money. Arlen had taken up the art of burglary a year ago, just trying to feed himself. Houses that looked empty with no lights on or no auto in the drive seemed to beckon to him. He was 5 ft. 7 in. tall and weighed only 125 lbs—the perfect build to slip through a half open window.

Farm work didn't appeal to him, nor did any other type of work, really. Houses were his specialty, but occasionally he'd venture downtown around two or three in the morning and try some back doors to businesses.

Medford at 3:00 a.m. was quiet, just a few stray cats, and Arlen moved through the shadows of the street lights. The third door he tried was a clothing store owned by an older German couple, Gustav and Anna Gottlieb. The building was wood, old and weathered. After a little prying and jiggling, the back door popped opened.

Arlen found himself in a storeroom. He waited a few minutes for his eyes to adjust to the gloom, then moved cautiously and carefully through the racks of clothes until he came to another door. This one opened by just turning the knob, and Arlen was in Gustav's office.

The streetlight on Main Street cast a murky glow through the high dirty window. A few chairs, a file cabinet and a big wood desk silently greeted him as he made his way toward the desk. Only the big drawer on the bottom right side was locked. Using a wooden ruler, Arlen managed to pop the lock. Inside was a metal box, also locked. Getting nervous, Arlen decided it was time leave. He slipped back through the clothing racks to the back door, the metal box tucked under his arm.

Arlen did not drive an auto. He had never learned how to drive, and did not want to. His method of travel was the railroad, usually in an empty boxcar. At the rail-yard, a fist-sized stone and a rusty spike soon had the metal box open. Inside was the Gottlieb's petty cash, almost $400 in assorted bills. For a moment, Arlen had trouble catching his breath. His heart pounded and a slim line of drool escaped the corner of his mouth. He stuffed the money in his pants pockets and threw the box in the weeds by the track. His options now were endless.

In a few hours, the diners' would be open and he could eat a meal off a plate and drink coffee from a clean cup. Then he'd buy a train ticket to Milwaukee where more houses and businesses waited for him.

Gustav and Anna opened their store at eight every weekday morning, but always arrived at six to take early deliveries. Finding the cash box missing, they called the police. The officers did three things immediately. Check for stolen cars, notify the bus and train stations, and stop at the bakery for an energy boost.

The ticket seller at the railroad station had sold a ticket to a poorly dressed young man with a pocket full of money. The train had left about half an hour ago. The police called ahead to Marshfield, asking their police to search the train when it stopped.

The Medford Police Chief, Harry Thiessen, called Billy to let him know about the suspected burglar on the train. "I have two officers waiting at the train station to pick him up," Harry said.

Billy thanked him, thought about it for a minute, then left the office.

Arlen was hungry. When the train stopped at Abbotsford, he got off and walked a block to Freddie's cafe and ordered breakfast. Coffee, eggs, bacon and pancakes. The waitress gave him a hard look, sniffed and left. Arlen looked at his shirt and pants, realizing he had money now and could upgrade his wardrobe.

After his meal, Arlen left the cafe. A half block away was a men's clothing store. Entering, the smell of new clothing was intoxicating. Arlen bought new khaki pants, a blue and white checkered shirt and boots. After paying $12.50, he changed in one of the booths, leaving his old clothes behind.

It was after 9 o'clock when he got back to the train station, and the train had left. "The next train to Milwaukee is at three this afternoon," the clerk told him.

Arlen smiled. "No hurry, I'll be back at three."

Billy drove home at 10 o'clock. "Helen. I'm driving up to Abbotsford. Would you make me a sandwich and a thermos of iced tea?"

"Of course dear, but why are you going to Abbotsford?"

"To give a young man a ride back to Medford," Billy said laughing, and told her about the burglary. Billy knew the train schedules, and when the police did not get their suspect at the Marshfield train station, Billy already knew what had happened. Taking his iced tea, he got in his patrol car.

Arlen had a pleasant day wandering around town. He saw the new fire engine at the fire station, bought an apple at the grocer's and ate it as he walked. The new boots hurt his feet a little so he took a break sitting on a bench in the park. Around noon he was back at Freddie's cafe for lunch. Meat loaf, mashed potatoes and gravy and green beans. The waitress remembered him because he left no tip. At a quarter to three he was back at the train station, ready to see Milwaukee.

Billy sat in the waiting room at the train station reading a newspaper and watching the people come and go. When Arlen walked in, Billy knew he had his man. The new clothes still showed store creases and the boots squeaked.

Billy walked up to Arlen ad held out his hand. "Hello, my name is Billy."

Smiling, Arlen held out his hand, and Billy snapped a handcuff on it! Arlen was not a fool or a fighter. Knowing he had been caught, he held out his other hand to be cuffed.

They talked as Billy drove to Medford, mostly about Arlen's past life and his present situation. "Will I go to jail?" Arlen asked.

"I'm certain you will," Billy said. "Have you been there before?"

"Just once, for vagrancy in Phillips," Arlen told him, "but it was only for ten days."

"This time it will be longer," said Billy. At Medford, the police were astounded. Waving them off, Billy said, "He's just a down-on-his-luck dumb kid. Take it easy on him." Then Billy was back in his patrol car and headed home.

Wayne and Lyle had just come back from patrol when Billy returned to Marshfield. Billy told them about Arlen and the burglary. He called Harry Thiessen and related the whole story. "The kid was lucky it was you who figured it out. You saved a lot of people a lot of wasted time and effort. Thanks again, Billy."

Ever so slowly the quart jar filled, and Joe capped it. It was late evening at the Gandt's, the stockpile of grain and molasses was getting low. Joe would get more at the feed store tomorrow. "Four quarts today," Joe told Louis, "only sixteen to go."

CHAPTER TWENTY-FIVE

Wayne watched Cassie sitting beside him in the car. It was Sunday afternoon, the first weekend of September. Like everyone who has ever grown a backyard garden, they both had planted too much of one thing and not enough of another. Wayne and Cassie drove out of town looking for the roadside produce stands that popped up like mushrooms in the early fall. Neither had planted enough potatoes, rutabaga's or onions and neither had an apple tree.

"There's one," Cassie said pointing at a stand with baskets and bags of potatoes. They stocked up, buying two fifty lbs. Of spuds and a 10 lb. bag of onions. Three miles later another stand yielded a basket of rutabaga's. The wooden bins in their basements would store these treasures through the winter. Turning down another dirt road they found a stand selling apples and pears. The Studebaker sat low on the springs when they finally got home.

Wayne ate supper at the Andersons. Helen made a hearty split pea with ham soup, one of Billy's favorites. Cassie and Wayne did the dishes, then went for an evening walk.

"Edna has asked me to be her maid of honor at the wedding," Cassie said.

Wayne grinned. "Lyle asked me to be his best man. I was the one who told him to stop at the diner to meet Edna."

"Did you think then that they would like each other?"

"I wasn't sure. It just seemed like a good idea."

"That really is a lovely ring he gave her," Cassie said. "Did you help him pick it out?"

"No, he did that by himself. Fortunately I will never have to select one for you."

Stunned, Cassie stopped and looked at him. "Just what do you mean by that?" Cassie said with an edge to her voice.

Wayne reached into his pants pocket and took out a small ring with a diamond set in. Holding it out to Cassie he said softly, "Because, my love, this engagement ring belonged to my mother." Wayne took her hand in his. "I have loved you even before I knew it was love. Will you marry me Cassie Anderson?"

Tears glistened in her blue eyes as Wayne slipped the ring on her finger. Cassie put her arms around Wayne's neck and drew him close until their noses touched. "Yes, I will marry you, Wayne Schooley. I have been waiting for this moment since you first walked me to school." They kissed long and slowly, letting their beating hearts express their joy. The full moon cast an ethereal glow on the young lovers as they embraced.

Even when you are expecting something wonderful you are still surprised when it happens. Billy and Helen Anderson had been waiting, and now the moment was here. Helen cried and hugged Cassie as Billy shook Wayne's hand.

"I am so happy for the two of you," Helen sobbed.

Billy hugged his daughter. "I knew he was going to ask you, but I didn't know when."

"Billy is hiding a small bottle of brandy somewhere to celebrate this moment aren't you dear?" Helen laughed.

Billy went to the closet and dug deep into his winter coat pocket. "Get some glasses, Helen, and we'll drink a toast to the happy couple." The clink of glasses and 'congratulations' echoed throughout the room.

"We must talk to Lyle and Edna," Cassie insisted, "our wedding dates must be at least a month apart."

Wayne and Cassie agreed they wanted to be married in the spring. "It gives everyone time to make plans and prepare," Wayne said.

"I guess Jan will be out of a job," said Billy.

"Oh no," Cassie insisted. "With Wayne and I both working, I want Jan to stay on as long as she wants."

"When I first came home it was Jan who helped me settle in," Wayne stated. "She has become like family. I agree, she can be with us as long as she wishes."

The next morning, Wayne told Jan about the engagement. She laughed, cried a bit and said, "Cassie is right. You'll need me to help while you both work. I'm so happy for you! I just knew that first kiss would bring the two of you together."

Laughing, Wayne answered, "And you were right! She never did slap me!"

"Edna was right," Lyle said when Wayne gave him the good news, "She said you would propose to Cassie by the end of August. I don't know how she knew, but she did."

"The four of us have to get together and make plans," Wayne said.

Laughing Lyle said, "The *four* of us will meet, but Cassie and Edna will make the plans."

The mornings were cooler and arrived a few minutes later each day. The flies and mosquito's bothered less each day as their numbers decreased. Spider webs that were brushed away did not reappear. Autumn was coming, bringing colorful changes to every corner of the state. Hunting seasons were starting, pheasant, grouse, ducks, geese and soon bear and deer. The wild game would supplement the diets of families in town and on the farm.

It was coal that now fueled most of the homes and businesses in Marshfield during the winter months. On the farms, it was wood. Logs hauled home from woodlots were sawed into lengths and split into firewood for the furnace or fireplace, and for the kitchen range to cook the food. The hard woods—oak, maple, elm and ash—were cut and stacked by the cord to fight off the winter cold. Soft woods, like spruce, were split easily into kindling for starting the kitchen stove. September was the month to prepare for winter, the month to harvest and reap what was sown.

CHAPTER TWENTY-SIX

Francis 'Patch' Mcleary was stockpiling whiskey. A small time hoodlum, Francis had been raised on the southeast side of Milwaukee. A knife fight when he was 14 had taken his left eye. The empty socket was covered with a patch, hence the nickname. He now stood at 6-foot tall and weighed 175 pounds, none of it fat. He always wore a bowler hat with a gray band and usually had a cigar in his mouth.

Francis ruled over a gang of street thugs, but with prohibition coming, he expected to finally break into the ranks of the real mob bosses. "Dapper" Danny Hogan from Minnesota and Dion "Deeny" O'Banion of Chicago were his hero's. All he needed was just one big break to make the big time. He'd been buying bootleg whiskey for months, storing it in a warehouse on Chelsea Street. When the 'no booze' law went into effect in 1920, 'Patch' would be ready.

Visiting day at the jail was Wednesday, and Joe was there to see his dad, Rodney. They sat at one of the picnic tables in the side yard.

"How many quarts?" Rodney asked.

"190," Joe answered, "one more week and I'll have the 200."

"In my small dresser drawer is a notebook with phone numbers," Rodney said softly. "One number is to 'Fats' in Milwaukee. He works for Patch McLeary. Call him and tell him you have the shipment ready."

"How will I deliver it?"

"You won't have to deliver, they will pick it up."

Joe let out a sigh of relief. He'd been dreading the trip to Milwaukee, fearing their old pickup would break down along the way. "I'll call him tomorrow," Joe said.

About a mile outside the Marshfield city limits was a hobo jungle. The train tracks were on the west side of the city. Heading north, the tracks went round a gentle curve and went over the Sandy Creek trestle and in the shadow of the bridge was a flat piece of land. Either coming or going, the train had to slow for the curve, making it an ideal spot to jump on or off a boxcar.

A heavy old wood crate had been found somewhere and held an array of pots, pans, tin cups, forks and spoons. A fire ring had been built with stones and large pieces of wood served as chairs. It seemed there was always a hobo around, but seldom the same one two days in a row. A big blue enamel coffee pot sat on a flat rock just inside the fire ring. The food was brought in by the men, and you shared what you had. The rule was 'no whiskey in the jungle.' Drinking caused fights, then the cops showed up.

Calvin Jones was from Kansas City, had been in the U.S. Marine Corps during the great war, and had seen and done things no young man should ever have to see or do. Returning home he found it difficult to settle down. He was restless and troubled. He began drinking to escape the drudgery of work, eat, sleep, then do it again day after day. With no family to hold him he decided to travel.

With no money, an empty boxcar became his home, and a day's work for cash would buy food. America was full of small hobo jungles, stretching from Boston to San Diego. Many were rough, filthy places inhabited by angry men. Calvin tried to stay clear of the worst ones, as they seldom had food to share. He drank less because whiskey cost money.

September found him traveling from Duluth-Superior where he had helped load the ore boats in the harbor. He carried a canvas bag containing his few possessions and a few cans of food. Harvest time was coming and when that was over he'd head south for the winter. Another hobo had told him about the camp at Marshfield, Calvin would reach it about sundown, stay the night and move on.

Billy had told Wayne and Lyle about the place. "They run a clean camp," Billy told them, "and most will give the local farmers a good days work for a few dollars and some food."

"Have they ever caused any trouble?" Lyle asked.

"Years ago, I posted a sign there saying: 'no whiskey allowed.' To this day, the sign is still there, and there has never been any trouble. Just check it now and then; the best time is early evening when you're on your back to the office."

There is no elegant or safe way to exit a moving boxcar. You jumped and hoped for the best, which is what Calvin did.

After picking himself up, he walked down the embankment to the camp. Two men were there drinking coffee. One of the men was 'Old Nick' who was close to fifty years old. He and Calvin had been in hobo camps together before. The other man was about thirty, and friendly.

He held out his hand. "I'm Ben, nice to meet you."

Calvin shook his hand. "I've got a big can of beans in my bag, enough for all three of us, if you'd care to join me." Ben went to the box and got a pan while Calvin opened the beans. The can would be washed out in the creek and go in the box later.

Wayne parked his patrol car, got out and walked down to the camp. Calvin tensed up, expecting to be rousted. Old Nick stood up, smiling. "Hi deputy, want some coffee?"

"Maybe half a cup," Wayne said.

Nick poured, handed him the cup and asked, "Any work to be had for a few days?"

Wayne sipped the hot brew. "Farmers are doing a third crop hay cutting, they would welcome some help. Tell them Wayne sent you." Wayne gave them directions to the farms, shook Nick's hand and left.

Calvin could not believe what he had just seen! When the patrol car drove away, he asked, "Was I dreaming, or did the law just offer to help us?"

Grinning, Old Nick pointed at the 'no alcohol' sign and said, "The sheriff put that sign up years ago. As long as we behave and don't bring no whiskey here, the sheriff and his deputies don't bother us. In fact, they sometimes help us find work."

Ben had watched the whole thing with his mouth open.

"I never seen the like," he said, "the law helping hobo's. It just ain't natural."

The beans were ready and as the men ate, they talked of other camps in other states. They agreed that Texas and California were the worst. Detroit, Chicago and new York were cities to avoid, Miami and new Orleans were good but only in the winter. As the night closed in the men chose a spot and slept.

All three found work pitching hay. The weather was good and the barns filled with the much needed cutting. The noon meals offered plenty of food and after three days the work was done. As they were paid they were told that the corn harvest would be ready in October if they were interested. Calvin was, and he said he would be back. He found he liked the work. It was outdoors and the farms he worked for treated him well. It seemed the call of the rails was getting fainter, not gone completely, but fainter. Maybe it was time to take stock of his life and what lay ahead.

Early the next morning over coffee, Old Nick told Ben and Calvin, "I'm headed down to Lake Geneva. There is some truck farms harvesting , if you want more work."

"Not me," Ben said. "I'm going to Kentucky."

"I'll go, Nick," Calvin said. "Let's go."

CHAPTER TWENTY-SEVEN

Dennis Mahoney had been a chubby baby who grew into a chubby child. The gang of boys he grew up with in Racine teased him, calling him 'fatso.' The extra weight followed him into his teen years, by which time he was called 'fats.' An incident at a pool hall left the owner with a broken arm. Only one of the gang was caught because he didn't run fast enough, being overweight. Dennis 'Fats' Mahoney went to reform school for three years. A meager diet of poorly cooked food, hard work and just trying to stay alive leaned down the excess weight Dennis carried, and at age 18 he emerged from the reform school a 5 ft. 10 in. well-muscled man with a distaste for law and order. He was recruited by Patch McLeary to carry out any assignment given to him. Lately he had been buying and storing whiskey at the Chelsea Street warehouse.

Fats reported to Patch about the phone call he had received. "A guy in Marshfield named Gandt says he has 200 quarts of home brew for sale at five dollars a quart. Are we buying?"

Patch lit his cigar, thought a minute, then said, "Let him

stew for a week or so, then offer him four dollars a quart. If he agrees, you take the truck and go get it."

Smiling, Fats said, "I like the way you do business."

Rodney Gandt was in pain. He woke up with a spasm of pain across his chest. Sitting up, he took a few deep breaths and waited for the pain to pass. It lessened, but did not go away. He told the jailer when they bought him breakfast. "Probably just gas," the jailer told him, and left. Not really hungry, Rodney just sipped his coffee. Moving around seemed to help some, but the pain nagged at him until noon.

At lunch, he told the jailer, "I want to see sheriff Billy." About one o'clock Rodney's left arm began going numb, and the pain swept across his chest. Billy got to the cell just as Rodney dropped to his knees clutching his chest.

"Call the hospital," Billy yelled. "This man is having a heart attack! Have them send an ambulance!" Rodney gasped for air, unable to talk. "Help is coming," Billy told him. "Just keep breathing." Minutes later a doctor and two orderlies rushed in, got Rodney on a stretcher and carried him out.

Wayne checked into the office as the ambulance was leaving. Billy told him what happened. "Go out to the Gandt place and let the boys know," Billy said, "I'll go see how Rodney is doing."

Wayne left in a hurry, knowing time was crucial. As he drove into the Gandt's drive, Louis was just coming out of the front door. "Go get your brother Joe and get up to the hospital," Wayne said, "your father just had a heart attack."

Joe had been standing just inside the door and gave Louis a shove. "Go get in the truck," he said.

Turning to Wayne he hollered "You lead the way deputy, I'll be right behind you."

Rodney lay on the bed, sweating and barely alive. Old Doctor Wallis leaned over him, pressing a stethoscope to his chest. "The heart is beating, but very irregular," he said. As he listened, he suddenly stood up. "The heart has stopped," he exclaimed. Young Doctor Sloan didn't hesitate. He grabbed the bedside lamp, pulled the plug from the wall, then pulled the cord from the lamp. He twisted the bare ends of the cord into prongs. Taking the nurse by the arm he instructed her. "When I tell you, plug this cord into the outlet. Leaning over Rodney, he pressed the two ends of the cord against the area of the heart.

"Plug it in," he said.

The nurse hesitated.

"Now!" shouted the doctor. "Do it now!"

With trembling fingers the nurse plugged in the cord. THUMP! Rodney's body lifted from the bed, then dropped back down. Doctor Wallis quickly leaned over with his stethoscope, pressing it to Rodney's chest. As he listened, his eyes got very wide. "The heart is beating again," he said in wonder, "and now the beat is regular!"

"Please unplug the cord," Doctor Sloan instructed the nurse. Staring at the young doctor with awe, the older man asked, "Where did you ever learn that?"

"I was working at a hospital in France during the war," Doctor Sloan said, "a French doctor there believed that electrical current could restart a human heart. This was the first time I ever had the opportunity to test the theory. Thank God, it works!"

When Louis and Joe arrived at the hospital, Rodney was breathing on his own and his heart beat was regular. His eyes were open and he could talk in a whisper. The boys were allowed one minute with their dad, then Rodney was moved to intensive care for the night.

"You boys go home now" Doctor Wallis told them, "if there is any change we will call you." As Joe and Louis left, Doctor Wallis reached into the pocket of his white smock and took out the lamp cord he had taken from the emergency room.

"What's that for?" Billy asked. The old doctor told Billy the story of how electricity had saved Rodney's life.

"I'm going to write a letter to the Medical Association and tell them of this miracle. If it can save lives, it must be perfected and used."

The next morning, the Marshfield newspaper carried the headline: 'DOCTOR SAVES LIFE WITH ELECTRICITY.' Cassie brought the paper home from work and showed Helen.

"Isn't it wonderful how something we take for granted now is able to save lives," Helen marveled.

They were sitting at the kitchen table having a late afternoon cup of tea. With a little smile, Cassie said, "The ambulance we now take for granted was the idea of an American Doctor at a field hospital in France. He wanted a way to bring the wounded from the battlefield to the hospital as quickly as possible."

Staring wide-eyed, Helen said, "I never realized that."

Nodding her head, Cassie said, "New techniques for setting broken bones, stronger, more effective antiseptics. Boiling surgical equipment, all these things came from the war. It's like a blessing wrapped in a curse."

Wayne and Lyle were in Billy's office after patrol. Billy held up a letter from St. Joseph's Hospital. "This letter says that Rodney must remain in the hospital for two months due to his fragile condition."

"Is the sheriff's office being held responsible for his condition?" Lyle asked.

"Doctor's Wallis and Sloan agree that being in jail had nothing to do with his heart attack," Billy stated. "It was a condition that built up over time and finally happened. In fact, Rodney was lucky it happened here. If he had been home, he would have died."

"That leaves Joe in charge of all that whiskey," Wayne said. "I wonder what they plan to do now."

Grinning, Billy answered, "The sheriff's grapevine says a guy in Milwaukee named McLeary is buying up all the whiskey he can get his hands on. I'm wondering if he has talked to Joe."

"Something should shake loose soon," Lyle said. "Let's keep checking on Joe. When he starts getting really nervous, we'll know the sale is about to happen."

CHAPTER TWENTY-EIGHT

The rain lasted for three days. Sometimes it was just a misty drizzle, then a downpour, then back to a light shower. Lyle got his patrol car stuck on a gravel road south of town. A half hour walk to the nearest farmhouse left him soaked. The farmer hitched his team and soon had Lyle back on the road. The sun was not visible through the gray clouds as the days passed. Then overnight the clouds lifted and in the morning the sun returned, and the late September winds helped dry out the landscape.

Wayne parked his car, got out, opened the rear door and took out a box from the rear seat. As he walked in the front door he called, "Jan, I've got a surprise for you!"

Jan hollered back, "Bring it in the kitchen."

Setting the box on the kitchen table, Wayne said, "The hardware store just got these in today." He opened the box and removed a square metal box with two rectangular holes in the top and a lever on the side. An electric cord was attached to the back of the box.

Staring at it, Jan asked, "What is it?"

"It's an electric toaster," Wayne said. "I'll plug it in and you cut two slices of bread from that loaf you baked yesterday."

Jan got out the bread and a knife, stared at the toaster a minute judging the size of the slices she needed. Wayne picked up the slices of bread, dropped them into the slots and pressed the lever down. The toaster hummed as it warmed up and the odor of warm bread filled the air.

"I'm timing how long it takes to toast the bread," Wayne said as he stared at the clock on the wall. About two and a half minutes later the lever sprang up and the toast popped halfway out of the toaster. Both Wayne and Jan stared at the toast a moment, then Wayne lifted the slices out and handed one to Jan. Her face broke into a smile and she laughed.

"I like it," she said. "Anything that makes life easier in the kitchen is fine with me."

On the morning of October 2nd, the Marshfield newspaper headline read: PRESIDENT SUFFERS MASSIVE STROKE! Woodrow Wilson was being monitored by a legion of doctors at Bethesda Naval Hospital. His re-election campaign was put on hold. People were not happy with Wilson, the federal tax he had bulldozed through congress to pay for the war had the nation ready for a new leader.

Joe Gandt was visiting Rodney that afternoon and showed him the headline. "Guess I ain't the only one with problems," muttered Rodney.

"Doctor says you got to stay here seven more weeks," said Joe.

"Better than sitting in that jail cell," Rodney answered. "No word from Fats, yet?"

"Not yet, but I expect he'll call soon," said Joe.

"About time to shut down the small still for winter," Rodney said softly. "Nights are getting colder."

"I'll give it a few more weeks," Joe said, "then take it apart and store it in the house. Louis won't like it, but if it freezes, the coil will bust open."

"Do what you gotta do son," Rodney said with some pride. "You're the boss now."

Standing in the parking lot by the Sheriff's office, Wayne and Lyle heard the odd noise. It sounded like an angry bee with a bad cold. A steady buzzing, then a series of coughs and more buzzing. They both looked up in surprise! An airplane was slowly circling as it descended, heading for a bare hayfield just south of town. They jumped into Wayne's patrol car and drove, trying to keep the airplane in sight. They arrived just as the pilot set the plane down on the bumpy ground. A few more coughs and sputters, and the engine quit.

A young man in a leather flying helmet and leather jacket climbed out of the cockpit onto the wing and jumped to the ground as the patrol car pulled up. The pilot was smiling as he took off the helmet and held out his hand.

"Hi fellas, I'm Allen Jessup," he said. "Hope I didn't scare you, but Jenny here ran out of gas."

They shook hands and Wayne said, "I saw these planes in the air over in France, but never saw one up close."

Lyle just stared at the plane in awe.

"Is there someplace nearby I can get some fuel?" Allen asked. Lyle started chuckling, then he laughed!

"What's so funny?" Wayne asked.

"I will buy you ten gallons of gas, if you will give my girlfriend a ride in your plane," Lyle said. "I will go get the gas, call her from the Standard station and have her drive out here."

Now Wayne started laughing! "All Edna talks about is someday riding in an airplane."

Allen's face split into a wide grin as he replied, "you have a deal! Go call the lady and tell her that plane ride is waiting!" Lyle left in a shower of gravel. Wayne walked around the plane as Allen told him about it. "This is a JU-4 Curtiss biplane," he said with pride. "It was built in July of 1918. Before they could even get it on a ship to France, the war was over!"

"Does it use a lot of fuel?" Wayne asked.

"Actually, it's really good on fuel, but occasionally it's a long trip between stops."

"I drove a supply truck in the war," Wayne said, "and would watch the planes overhead. Most were British, a few French."

"I didn't get overseas," Allen said, "I got out of flight school just as the war ended."

"Where are you flying to now?"

"The last air show of the year starts in two days in Minneapolis, and I do stunt flying with three other pilots."

Lyle returned with two five gallon cans full of fuel. As Allen finished fueling up, A Model-T roared up with Edna driving. She stared wide-eyed at the plane, then at Allen, and finally at Lyle.

"Are you ready for your long awaited plane ride?" Lyle

asked with a big grin.

"I didn't believe it when you called," Edna said breathlessly, "but here it is, an airplane!"

As she got out of the car, all three men gave a little laugh and pointed at her. Looking down, Edna realized she still had her apron on! Whipping it off, she laughed too. She gave Lyle a hug. "OK. How do I get into this machine?"

With Allen's help, she was soon sitting in the second seat. "Buckle your seat belt," Allen said, and started the engine. He swung the tail of the plane around and took off down the field.

Allen did some easy loops and once flew upside down. After 15 minutes he landed. Edna was laughing, probably the happiest girl in Marshfield at that moment. As Wayne and Lyle helped her from the plane, Allen asked "I'll be glad to give you men a turn also." Both agreed, and Lyle went next, then Wayne. After dropping Wayne off, Allen waved, sped off down the field and became a speck in the sky. After a long hug, Edna gave Lyle a kiss, got in her Ford and went back to work.

When he got home that evening, Cassie was there with Jan. Wayne told them about the plane and Edna. Cassie laughed so hard she had tears in her eyes. Jan wanted to know all about the plane and how it worked.

"Let's have supper, and I'll tell you all about it," said Wayne. Jan had made a New England style boiled dinner with pork. Wayne tried to explain to Jan how a plane could fly, and how it stayed in the air.

"My bicycle gets me around just fine," she said, "so I think I will just stick with that."

CHAPTER TWENTY-NINE

He wanted to go back to Marshfield. Calvin Jones could not explain it to himself or Old Nick why the town seemed to have a hold on him, but it did. The farm he thought about was the Schumacher's. The older couple had treated him well, even given him some clothing that had belonged to their son who had been killed in the war.

"Sometimes, life is what it is," Old Nick told him, "if that's what your heart tells you to do, best do it." Nick was going south to Arkansas. "Can't take the cold like I used to. By December I'll be in New Orleans."

They parted ways and Calvin caught a freight train going north.

The first frost had been light, the second was harder. The corn was ready to cut. The corn binders were dragged out of the machine sheds and made ready. Some would be pulled by teams of horses, others by tractor. The trick was finding just the right speed to cut. As the stalks were cut, the binder rolled the stalks into sheaves, which then dropped out the back or side, depending on the brand of binder. Teams of two men each stacked the sheaves into shocks, usually five sheaves to a shock. Later, the shocks would be loaded on a wagon and taken to the farm. The ears were cut from the stalks and husked. The stalks were cut up for silage and fed to the cows. The ears of corn were shelled and bagged to be sold or used.

Wayne slowed the patrol car down when he saw the man walking along the road the next morning. As he pulled up alongside, he recognized Calvin Jones.

"Good morning," Wayne said. "Can I give you a lift?"

"Thanks," Calvin said as he got into the car, "I'm going out to the Schumacher farm to see if they need help with the corn harvest."

"I remember they asked you to come back," said Wayne. "I'm sure they can use the help."

When the patrol car stopped in the farmyard and Calvin got out, Virginia hurried out of the house with a big smile, wiping her hands on her apron. "Mr. Calvin Jones," she said. "I am so glad you came back. Dan starts cutting corn tomorrow and another good hand is welcome." Gesturing toward the house, she added, "Wayne, you and Calvin come in for some coffee and fresh biscuits, and I won't take no for an answer."

Virginia Schumacher took great pride in showing off the new house that Hiram Peterson had built. A big airy kitchen with two windows, a countertop with a white enamel sink and a hand pump. The new Belvedere cook range with reservoir and warming oven dominated one wall. Dan sat at the kitchen table as they entered.

"Take a chair and sit" he said, "good to see both of you. Glad you came back Calvin. Ginnie and I were hoping you would."

Ginnie set down two cups of coffee. "Dan and I were talking this morning about you, Calvin," she said with a smile, "we hoped you would return and help with the corn. Also, we hoped for more. I'll let Dan ask you."

Clearing his throat, Dan looked directly at Calvin and said, "since I'm not getting any younger, there are times when I need help running the farm. Ginnie and I have decided we need to hire a young man to help out. Our son Jacob was killed in the war. I wish you could have known him; he was a fine young man."

Seeing that Dan was stumbling for words, Ginnie said, "you remind us both of Jacob, which we find comforting. We would like to hire you full time, to help us run the farm."

"We have two spare bedrooms upstairs," Dan said, "I know there is a lot to learn, but I have plenty of time to teach you all about farming." Calvin had sat quietly sipping his coffee. Setting his cup down, he looked at Ginnie, then Dan and finally Wayne.

"I *am* tired of traveling," he said. "I want to do something with my life. I like the peace and quiet of the mornings, the harvesting, the animals and the sense of belonging." Looking at Wayne he said "You were the one who first sent me out here, and I am grateful." Turning to Ginnie he smiled. "Can we have biscuits every morning?" The house filled with laughter.

Wayne left feeling the way a man does after a good deed has been done. A swelling in the chest, a lightness of the heart and a feeling of accomplishment. 'Wait till I tell Cassie about this,' he thought.

Patrolling northeast of Marshfield, Lyle passed several farms harvesting corn. He parked on the side of the gravel road and walked to the cornfield. A man and woman were shocking corn. "Good morning deputy," the man said. "How can we help you?"

"I wonder if I might buy one of those sheaves," Lyle said.

With a puzzled look, the woman asked "Whatever would you do with it?"

"My fiancé, Edna, at Daryl's Diner wants to decorate their front porch with cornstalks and pumpkins," Lyle said, blushing.

The woman laughed and said, "We know the Weber family. We heard their daughter got engaged. Congratulations!" Taking one of the sheaves, she handed it to Lyle. "You can't buy one if I give it to you," she said with a grin. "Tell Daryl and Patti hello from the Felkers."

"Will you stop that walking through the house? It's making me nervous," Louis told Joe. Waiting for Fats to call back made Joe anxious. When the phone rang, Joe ran to pick it up. "Hey kid, this is Fats. The boss says we can buy your whiskey at $4 a quart." Joe knew if he argued, the deal might be off.

"Dad says four is good," Joe told Fats. "When can you pick it up?"

"It'll be a few days," Fats said. "The truck is on its way to

Thunder Bay, Canada. I'll call you when they get back. You just have the booze ready to go."

At the hospital, Rodney agreed with Joe. "$800 is better than nothing," he said, "It should cover the hospital bill with a little left over."

"You just rest easy, Dad," Joe said. "I'll take care of everything."

That evening Wayne and Cassie were in Carson's cafe with Lyle and Edna. They had all been to the theater to see the movie 'The Outcast of Poker Flats,' starring Harry Carey and Gloria Hope. Over coffee and pie they talked of their upcoming weddings. "Lyle and I have decided to have our wedding the first Saturday in May," Edna said, "With just a few days for a short honeymoon."

"That will work out great," Cassie said excitedly. "Wayne and I picked the last Saturday in May!" As the girls chattered on about flowers and dresses, Lyle told Wayne his plans.

"Dad has started remodeling our house," he said. "He says a new wife deserves a new kitchen and bathroom."

"It might be a good idea for you to stay with me while Hiram is working on your place." Wayne said. "I've got the spare room and you won't miss a meal." All four agreed it would be best. "I'll tell Jan in the morning. Having one more to cook for will make her happy."

CHAPTER THIRTY

The Wood County Farmers Cooperative was having their Annual Harvest Ball at the Marshfield town hall. Notices were posted all over the county inviting members to attend. Music would be provided by the Freddie Bayliss Polka Band. The Ladies Aid Society would have a bake sale and door prizes would be awarded. This was the fifth year the Cooperative held the ball, and membership had grown. Farmers could buy their seeds and supplies in bulk from companies and save money. Members got a better price for their milk and eggs. A monthly newsletter advertised animals and machinery for sale statewide. The Harvest ball was the cooperative's way of thanking folks for their support.

The aroma from the kitchen made Wayne's mouth water. Jan was baking pies for the Ladies Aid bake sale. A peach pie and an apple pie sat on the counter, and a pumpkin pie and another apple pie were in the oven.

"One apple pie is for dessert." Jan said, "The rest are spoken for."

Grinning, Wayne asked "Was there time for making supper?"

Laughing, Jan said, "I made chicken noodle soup for you and Lyle. It's ready when you are." Lyle came into the kitchen from the back door carrying an armload of wood for the cookstove. "I'm not much good at cooking," he said, "so I make up for it with a saw and an axe."

As they ate, Jan brought them up to date on all the news. "The President's doctor says Wilson is paralyzed on his left side, but his mind is clear," Jan said, "But the newspapers say his wife Edith is really running the country. She won't let anyone in to see the President except the doctor."

"I know Wilson was against prohibition," Lyle said. "He vetoed the bill, but congress overrode him and voted it in."

"I'm afraid the Volstead act is going to cause more problems than it solves," Wayne added. "Criminals will find a way to profit from it."

Barney Hauser was on the run. For months he had been skimming money from 'The Rose' nightclub in Milwaukee. The new Pierce Arrow he was driving was going to take him to Canada where he planned to get lost in the crowd. $15,000 was in the leather case on the passenger seat, right next to the model 1911 Colt .45.

He had left Milwaukee around midnight, with a good three hour head start, and if his luck held he should make Duluth/Superior in 12 to 14 hours, depending on the roads. Also, most of the gas stations didn't open until six AM. In Watertown he waited a half an hour at the standard station until the owner arrived. Gassing up, he drove northwest. A quick breakfast at a diner and back on the road. By noon he was having trouble keeping his eyes open. At a roadside park outside Baraboo he took a nap for an hour then stopped for a sandwich. He refueled at Tomah and continued northeast.

The Rose was owned by the Aiello family, and two men in a Packard were already on Barney's trail. He had bragged to a pretty waitress about someday retiring in Canada. "A man can get lost there and never be found," were his words. Within two hours, not three, the Packard drove on through the night. Two five gallon cans of gasoline were tied down in the trunk. These men had been on the road before. By noon they were a half hour behind Barney and closing.

Barney refueled at a station on the southern end of Eau Claire. He tucked the .45 into his belt, covering it with his jacket. Taking the bag of money with him, he entered the station and paid. He heard two car doors slam and turned to look out the door. Two men in dark suits had gotten out of a Packard and were walking toward the door. One man was average height and stocky. The other was tall and thin. The thin man had his right hand in his coat pocket.

Barney knew who they were and was surprised they had found him so quickly. He pulled his Colt from his belt with his right hand, grabbed his leather bag with his left hand and stepped out the door, shooting! The stocky man had been reaching for the pistol in his belt when Barney's first shot blew out his heart. The thin man got off one shot with a .38 revolver as he went down, hitting Barney in the left side. Barney's shot was dead center in the thin man's chest. The station owner was yelling into his telephone, "Get the cops out here, some guys are killing each other!" Barney didn't wait. He jumped into his car and sped off.

The bullet that hit Barney had punctured his left lung and nicked a blood vessel. Barney drove east about ten miles, but the pain finally got the better of him and he turned off onto a dirt track, drove another half mile and stopped. He got out of the car and took a look at his wound. It was bleeding slowly, but steadily. He took off his shirt and undershirt. He needed something to cover the holes so he could drive. He took off his socks, placing them on his side, they covered both holes. Ripping open his undershirt he was able to wrap it around his waist and tie it, holding the socks in place.

As he bandaged himself, he came up with a desperate plan. They knew where he was headed, and would be waiting for him at Duluth/Superior. 'I'll drive to Sault Ste. Marie' he thought, 'they won't expect that.' He put his shirt back on, donned his jacket and drove back out to the highway. 'If I can make Marshfield,' Barney thought, 'I can have a doctor patch me up.'

The pain increased slowly and Barney was having trouble breathing. When he coughed, there was a pink tinge coming up. He was sweating heavily and was very thirsty, but desperation kept him going. He stopped once to check his wound, which continued to bleed. The blood vessel that had been hit by the bullet was slowly ripping open, sending less blood to his heart and gathering in his lung.

At midnight he crossed into Wood County. Ever so slowly Barney's body was shutting down. Finally after ten more agonizing miles the Pierce Arrow rolled to a stop at the side of the road. With one last bloody gasp, Barney Hauser died.

When Lyle and Wayne entered the office at seven in the morning, Billy was on the telephone. "My deputies just came in," he said, "I'll let them know." As he hung up, Billy told them, "Big shooting in Eau Claire yesterday. Two men dead, one wounded. The wounded man drove off. The sheriff there thinks he may be coming this way, so be careful."

Wayne spotted the Pierce Arrow parked by the side of the road. He pulled over, parked and got out of his patrol car. He could see someone sitting slumped over in the driver's seat.

"Get out of the car with your hands up," he yelled. When the man didn't move, Wayne slowly approached with his revolver drawn. The driver's window was open and the coppery smell of blood drifted from within. Wayne poked the man's shoulder with his pistol. By this time Wayne was sure the man must be dead. He opened the driver's door, felt for a pulse. Nothing.

CHAPTER THIRTY-ONE

Wayne drove to the nearest farmhouse a mile away to call Billy. "Stay there till I arrive," Billy said, "I'll have an ambulance take the body to the morgue." The ambulance arrived an hour later with Billy leading the way. Wayne helped get the body on a stretcher and into the ambulance. The driver left just as Snuffy Bigelow arrived with his tow truck.

"Snuffy, I want you to take this car to my office," Billy told him, "I want to look it over real good. Maybe I can piece together what happened."

Snuffy dropped the Pierce Arrow off at the far end of the gravel parking lot. Billy walked around the car slowly, looking for any damage or bullet holes. Finding none, he opened the passenger side door. On the floor sat the leather bag, beside it lay the Colt .45. Billy picked up the bag, set it on the passenger seat and opened it. Wayne was looking over Billy's shoulder and gasped when he saw the contents. Bundles of money, mostly tens and twenties held together with rubber bands.

"I think we found the reason for the shooting," Billy said, "I'll take the bag, you grab the pistol. We'll take them in the office and count the money."

"Almost $15,000 here" Billy said, "no reports of any bank robberies in the past week. I better call Eau Claire." The sheriff in Eau Claire was glad to hear about Wayne finding Barney and the car, but was puzzled about the money.

"He was headed northwest," the sheriff said, "either into Minnesota or possibly to Canada at Duluth/Superior."

"Probably Canada," said Billy, "Lots of wilderness up there. If anyone contacts you about the money, call me, then send them over here."

"You go back on patrol," Billy told Wayne, "I'm going to the morgue. I want to find out who that dead body is, that might tell me why he was shot."

At the morgue, the doctor explained to Billy how he died. "When that blood vessel opened up he just plain bled to death. The hole in his lung didn't help any."

"I need his personal effects: his clothes and whatever was in his pockets.

An attendant handed Billy a paper bag. "This is everything he had."

Back at the office, Billy laid an old newspaper on his desk and emptied the bag on it. Shoes, jacket, bloody shirt and pants, makeshift bandage, loose change, a matchbook, and a wallet. The driver's license was for Bernard T. Hauser, age 42 from Milwaukee. The matchbook was from 'The Rose' nightclub. Billy flipped the matchbook in the air and caught it. 'He tried to steal from the Aiello family and got caught,' thought Billy. He was certain he would get a call about the money very soon.

The Harvest Ball was that night, and it was a great success. Juniors and Seniors from the high school had helped to decorate the hall with streamers, balloons and bunting. Freddie Bayliss had brought two fiddlers along with his polka band to play some waltz's. A huge punch bowl was monitored closely by the temperance league and it took three tables to lay out all the cakes, pies and other desserts from the Ladies Aid Society.

Edna was surprised to learn that Lyle was a pretty fair dancer. He could polka and waltz with ease. Wayne was learning to polka, with chuckles and giggles from Cassie. Police Chief Harry Thiessen won a door prize: a bottle of blackberry brandy, donated by the volunteer firemen. Laughing he said "Now I suppose my entire force will come down with colds and want a shot to recover." By midnight folks were putting on their coats, shaking hands, hugging friends and going home.

The next morning, two men got off the early morning train from Milwaukee. A portly man of average height wearing a $500 suit and a bowler hat carried a briefcase. The other man was shorter, wore a $50 suit and a fedora hat. The portly man hailed Tom the taxi driver, asking, "Where's the sheriff's office?"

"I'll take you right there," Tom said. They arrived just as Billy was opening the door.

"How can I help you gentlemen?" Billy asked.

"We need a few moments of your time" said the portly man, "to settle a very important matter."

Entering the office, Billy pointed at the two chairs in front of his desk. "Have a seat and let's talk."

The portly man held out a white business card. "Antonio D'Costa, Attorney-at law," Billy read off the card.

"I represent the Aiello family of Milwaukee," Antonio said, "they wish to claim the body, the automobile, and all the personal effects of the deceased, Mr. Bernard Hauser."

"You are welcome to them," Billy said with a smile, "We have no further use for them." The paper bag of clothing sat on the corner of Billy's desk. Unlocking his file cabinet, he took the leather bag from the bottom drawer and handed it to Antonio. "Have you looked in the bag?" Antonio asked.

"We not only looked," Billy told him, "We counted the money. Almost $15,000 in small bills. His Colt .45 is in there also."

"That is the amount we expected," Antonio said, "Thank you for helping the family clear up this unfortunate matter. If you will direct us to the morgue, we will take the auto and be on our way."

"How will Mr. Hauser make it home?" Billy wondered.

"I will have the body shipped by rail to Milwaukee," Antonio said stiffly.

Wayne and Lyle were just coming in as the two men were leaving. They watched the them inspect the car, then Antonio got in the back, the driver in the front and they left.

"They sure didn't waste any time," Wayne said.

"Mr. Hauser is going home to his family, God rest his soul," Billy said.

CHAPTER THIRTY-TWO

Rodney Gandt was dressed and waiting for Billy at the front desk of St Joseph's hospital. In his hand he held a list of instructions from the doctor and his final bill. When Billy arrived, Rodney held out his hands, expecting handcuffs.

"We won't need the handcuffs, Rodney. In fact, I have some good news. Joe is waiting for us at the office."

Billy sat behind his desk with Rodney and Joe facing him. "I talked to Judge Tatum yesterday, and we agreed that because of your medical problems, the jail is not a place for recovery," Billy stated. "For the remainder of your sentence, you will be under house arrest."

"You mean I can go home?" Rodney said.

"Yes, you can," Billy said, "but you must remain there. I and my deputies will be checking on you daily. If you need to go to the hospital for any reason, we'll take you, otherwise you are confined to your home."

Rodney looked at Joe, who nodded his head, saying, "Better than sitting in a cell, Dad."

"Today, Joe will take you home," Billy said, "and there you must remain until your sentence is completed."

Rodney stood and held out his hand. "I know the Judge wouldn't go for this without your say so," Rodney said sincerely, "I won't let you down" he said shaking Billy's hand.

When Wayne and Lyle returned from patrol that afternoon, Billy told them about Rodney's house arrest. "They still have all that bootleg whiskey in the house," Wayne said, "I'll bet someone is coming to pick it up soon."

"When they do, we'll let them load it up and go," Billy said firmly.

"Why not be there to stop them?" Lyle asked.

Giving his deputies a long look, Billy explained. "The men coming for that whiskey are professional thugs, with guns. If we try to arrest them at Gandt's home, they will surely start shooting. I don't want any of the Gandt's or either of you getting shot."

"So what do we do?" Wayne asked.

"We do nothing," Billy answered. "We let them load the truck and drive away. My good friend Sheriff Jensen will stop them with a roadblock outside Watertown in Dodge County. I'll call and give him a description of the truck and what time they leave Marshfield."

"Why that far away?" Lyle wondered. "The distance will remove any connection to the Gandt's" said Billy, "This will be just a random stop by a local sheriff."

"Rodney will still be hundreds of dollars ahead," Wayne said.

Billy replied, "Rodney owes the hospital hundreds of dollars for his care. I would rather see the hospital get paid than some Federal Agency who would squander the money."

Nodding and smiling, Wayne and Lyle had to agree, it was a good plan.

On their way home, Joe told Rodney his good news. "Fats called yesterday, they are coming tonight to pick up the whiskey."

"I'll be glad to see it go," Rodney said. "Maybe my life can get back to normal."

"With the $800 we can build a new still in the spring," said Joe.

With a heavy sigh, Rodney said, "Our whiskey-making days are over Joe." Slowly Rodney handed Joe the hospital bill.

Taking a look, Joe's eyes got wide open. "This says you owe St. Joseph's $780! We will only have $20 left." Nodding his head, Rodney said "I made Billy a promise, so I have to pay it."

At 8 o'clock that night, Billy parked his car a half-mile up the road from the Gandt's. Taking his binoculars, he walked to a spot in the field where he could see the house lit by the yard light. At 8:30 a truck drove into the yard, turned around and backed up to the front door. A sign on the side of the truck read TEMPLE DELIVERY SERVICE. Smiling, Billy made his way back to his car and drove back to town.

Joe opened the door as Fats and his driver got out of the truck. "Let's hurry up and get this stuff loaded," Fats said, "You never know who is watching." It took only a half-hour to get all the boxes full of quart jars stacked and tied down in the truck. As the driver closed the rear door, Fats handed Joe an envelope.

Opening it, Joe counted eight one hundred dollar bills. "Pleasure doing business with you," Fats said. He and his driver got in the truck and drove away.

At eight o'clock the next morning Billy got a call from Sheriff Jensen in Watertown. "The truck you called me about got stopped last night two miles outside of town."

"Hope there wasn't any trouble," Billy said.

"One man dead, one wounded, none of them my men," Jensen told him. "We had a roadblock up, checking trucks. When the Temple Service truck got there, the driver tried to ram the roadblock while shooting his pistol out the window. One of my deputies fired two shots with his .45 and killed him. The truck rolled to a stop and the passenger got out shooting. Another deputy with a Springfield rifle put a 30.06 bullet in the passengers shoulder."

"Glad you all are in good shape" Billy said. "What about the whiskey?"

"Two federal guys are coming to get it today. I told them it was a random stop, and we just got lucky," Jensen said.

"That's one I owe you," Billy said. "Thanks again."

The Marshfield News obituary reported that Miss Evelyn Consadine had passed away at the age of 72. It told a brief story of her career as an elementary school teacher. There was no family to notify, she had never married. It gave information on where the funeral would be held and at what time. What it did not give was the legacy Miss Evelyn had left behind.

Evelyn had been born to Owen and Louise Consadine at home in 1848. Evelyn was an only child. Owen was a tailor, his shop was their home on Beacon Street. Evelyn was 13 when the Civil war began, her father joined the Wisconsin 2nd regiment and was killed at Vicksburg. Louise Consadine never remarried and worked as the town librarian until her death in 1870.

Evelyn worked her way through teachers College in Oshkosh, graduating two months before her mother's death. Evelyn's first and only teaching job was the elementary school in Marshfield. She taught English and History. She also helped shape the lives of every child who passed through her classroom. At lunch time, no child went hungry. Evelyn bought extra sandwiches with her for the children who had none. If a child were being abused at home, Miss Evelyn knew, and soon the sheriff paid the family a visit.

The children loved her because she was fair, honest and cared about them. Her students went on to become doctors, lawyers, bankers, judges, merchants, police and firemen and parents whose children were taught by Miss Evelyn. She often settled disputes between adults who once were her students. One of her closest and dearest friends was Judge Willard Tatum, who often asked her advice on delicate family issues.

Her health had been failing a year before she died. Her doctor and a nurse were sworn to secrecy so she could finish the school year, 'for the children,' she had told them.

The funeral home had no way of knowing that almost five hundred people would show up, each with their own 'Miss Evelyn' story. The church was overwhelmed as well, so many flowers arrived they reached to the alter and beyond. The town board ordered a marble headstone inscribed 'an educator without equal.' There were so many volunteers that names had to be drawn from a hat for six pallbearers. There was no wake because 'Miss Evelyn would not have approved.'

A scholarship committee would be formed to award a deserving student a further education 'in Miss Evelyn's name.' Wisconsin state senator Howard Van Dyne, a former student, gave the eulogy. Someone was heard to comment 'such a shame she never had children.' Senator Van Dyne replied "Miss Evelyn had hundreds of children, each one special, each one loved." Marshfield would always remember 'Miss Evelyn.'

CHAPTER THIRTY-THREE

The corn was harvested, and now the fall plowing would begin, followed by the disc harrow. The earth must be turned to make it ready for planting winter wheat. Farmers had learned from their fathers the importance of crop rotation to replenish the soil. Fertilizer from the barn would be spread in the winter. The tractor made farming go easier and faster, until something broke down. Almost every farm kept at least one team of horses, just in case.

All a horse needed was good shoes, and Justin Reinholt was the man to shoe them. Justin farmed on a small scale, with most of his crop going to feed his horses. His main occupation and source of income was blacksmithing. He had learned the trade from his father and grandfather. The forge was in use every day except Sunday.

The front yard was a mixture of repaired, and waiting to be picked up on one side of the drive, and broken, waiting to be fixed on the other. Lately, a lot of work was adapting horse-drawn equipment to tractor-drawn. Justin and his wife Nancy had eight horses of their own. Four Belgians and four Suffolks. A big attraction at any County fair was the horse pull, and Justin would be there with one team or the other. Justin was a six footer with biceps the size of most men's thighs. His wife Nancy was a sturdy five footer who could handle a team as good as Justin.

There is an art to shoeing horses, almost like a heavy duty dance step that man and horse are trained to do. Farmers often waited while their horses were shod, just to watch and marvel at the process. When asked if the tractor would put him out of business, Justin would smile and point out to his front yard. "The horse will always be with us," he would say, "and they will always need shoes."

Wayne made it a point to stop at the Reinholt farm whenever he was in the area. Nancy made the tastiest cinnamon rolls he had ever tasted. He drove into the yard, parked and saw Justin arguing with Darnell Minor. Walking toward them Wayne overheard Justin say, "I won't do any more work for you until you pay me for the last job."

Wayne had to smile, because everyone considered Darnell's full name as 'Darnell I'll-pay-you-next-time Minor.

"I just don't have the money right now," whined Darnell.

"You promised last time to pay me this time," Justin said holding firm.

Wayne stepped closer. "How much does he owe?"

"Five dollars," Justin said.

Looking at Darnell, Wayne said, "Pay the man Darnell, or I tell Billy you're up to your old tricks again." Darnell was over 50 years old and as tan as saddle leather, but at the mention of Billy's name, he went pale. Without another word, he pulled a five dollar bill from his pants pocket, handed it to Justin, got in his truck and left.

Smiling, Justin tucked the bill in his pocket, and patted Wayne on the back. "Your timing is as good as ever. Nancy just took a fresh pan of cinnamon rolls out of the oven. Let's go eat."

The remodeling at Lyle's house was half done. Hiram had the kitchen and bathroom gutted and started from scratch. New counter tops and cupboards in the kitchen with a new sink and hand pump. The floor would be varnished oak and the small window above the sink was replaced with a large rectangular one. The bathroom would get a new tub and shower, new window and a tile floor.

As he worked Hiram remembered his life with his late wife June in this house. He had been gone from home a lot because of his work, but tried to make up for it when he was home. Lyle had grown up here; now he and Edna would begin a new family here. Seeing them together swelled his heart with pride. Edna was the perfect match for Lyle. Hiram smiled to himself as he thought, 'I could be a grandpa in about a year.' The thought pleased him as he worked.

At the railroad yard, the cars of coal were being unloaded into waiting trucks for delivery to the businesses in Marshfield. It was all anthracite coal, the clean burning coal. The rumble of tons of coal being shoveled down chutes was a daily background noise mostly ignored by the customers. However, it did cause a fine black dust to settle over the town, but this was expected and daily cleaning removed most of it. Not many years before, it had been tons of hardwood that was burned through the winter. Some old timers still held with the wood burning method with 'Don't have all that damn black dust' as their reason. Many housewives opted for wood for cooking. Coal burned hotter, often burning a favorite dish. So, most houses still had a woodpile by the backdoor.

Lyle drove past the Lamplight Tavern on Deerkill road. It was closed, no lights burning inside. It was a two story building, the owners had lived upstairs. Now it looked deserted. It was the third tavern closed this week. The Simmons Tavern and grill on Cedar Road and the Monroe's Tavern had also closed. Prohibition was almost here.

The brewery in Marshfield had closed in September and would probably never reopen. The coming of the new law had consequences far beyond any lawmakers understanding. Entire families out of work, businesses closed, thousands of men now unemployed and the holidays fast approaching.

The Marshfield Volunteer Fire Dept. was getting two new trucks. A hook & ladder and a pumper. They had been purchased by the Army for use in France during the war. They had been loaded on a transport ship, the USS *Robert Hayes* in October 1918. They reached France on the first of November. The Captain of the *Robert Hayes* received word not to unload his cargo, because the Armistice was going to be signed. On November 15, the USS *Robert Hayes* again sailed, this time back to New York. It took months for the Army to inventory it's war surplus. Finally, it offered the Ford hook & ladder and pumper for sale at $500 total for the two trucks — the U.S. Army had paid $650 apiece.

A Wisconsin Senator called the Marshfield Mayor who then called an emergency meeting of the town board who passed a funding bill authorizing the purchase. Both trucks would be delivered by rail. It would take years for the war inventory to be sold off, and some great deals were to be had.

Lyle had made up his mind. He was at Harry Mason's car lot looking over a 1917 Buick Sedan. Harry, waiting nearby, asked, "Did you want to trade in the motorcycle?"

"What kind of deal can you make me if I trade it in?" Lyle asked.

Harry rubbed his chin. "Well, I know someone looking for a motorcycle and yours is in good condition, so I can let you have the Buick for $250 with a trade."

"I want Snuffy to look it over first," Lyle said.

"It just came from Snuffy's garage yesterday," Harry said, "He gave it an oil change and grease job. You can call him from the office if you want."

"I've got $225 in cash right now," Lyle said, "Take it or leave it."

With a big sigh, Harry threw his hands in the air saying, "Alright, I'll take it, I'll give you my deputy discount. Let's go do the paperwork."

Edna was not surprised to see Lyle drive up to the diner in his Buick. "I love it!" she yelled, "Let's go for a drive."

The car ran smooth and handled well. "I want to drive it," Edna said.

Knowing she had a heavy foot, Lyle replied, "Alright, but no speeding, I don't want to have to give you a ticket."

As she drove, Edna said "I know we'll miss the motorcycle, but this is more practical." With a sigh, Lyle just nodded his head.

CHAPTER THIRTY-FOUR

The office was always cold in the morning until Billy shoveled some coal in the stove and fired it up. As the office warmed, the police chief in Medford called. "One of our local hoodlums escaped jail last night. We're still looking for him, but I think he may have got on the train at five this morning."

"Does Abbotsford know yet?" Billy asked.

"I called them before I called you," the chief said. "His name is Clay Hanover, 17 years old, 5 ft. 10 inches tall, brown hair, wearing jeans and a gray, red and white plaid shirt. He was awaiting trial for stealing a truck."

"So, he may get off the train and steal another one," Billy said.

"If you apprehend him, just bring him back," said the chief. "It was my truck he stole."

Laughing, Billy assured him, "I'll escort him myself."

Clay had got on the train that had a flat-bed rail car had two big red fire trucks chained down on it. Climbing into the cab of one and relaxed as the train headed toward Abbotsford. He knew they might check the train for him, so he got off the train and tried thumbing a ride. A salesman drove him as far as Unity, then it was more walking. Another car pulled up alongside him, and Clay got in. The older man smiled and said. "A little cold to be walking son, where are you headed?"

"Going to see my uncle in Wisconsin Rapids," Clay said. "He might have a job for me."

"Perhaps you should make your court date in Medford first, Clay" Billy said. Clay's eyes got big and his jaw dropped. "I'm the Wood County Sheriff. Your police chief called me to be on the lookout for you."

Clay hung his head and slowly started laughing. "Just my luck to be picked up by a cop. Are you taking me back now?"

Turning his car around, Billy said, "Yep. And on the way back, you can tell me how you got in this mess."

"I rode with two other guys to a dance in Dorchester. I met this girl there and we really hit it off. She had borrowed her father's truck to get to the dance and offered me a ride back to Medford if I would drive. On the way back, two patrol cars blocked me in, so I stopped. The girl was the police chief's daughter and they were out looking for the truck. They took me to jail and she took the truck home."

Billy laughed so hard he could hardly drive. Finally, he told Clay, "I think I can get you out of this predicament. Do you really have an uncle in Wisconsin Rapids?"

"His name is Jerome Kearns." Clay said, "He's a logger for the paper mill."

"When we get to Medford, you be quiet, don't say one word," Billy told him. "I'll talk to the police chief, he owes me a favor."

Billy called in his favor, and Clay was released on the condition he leave town for good. Billy drove Clay to the bus station and bought him a one way ticket to Wisconsin Rapids. "Thanks for helping me," Clay said. "Someday I'll pay you back for the bus ride."

Billy shook his hand and said, "Just stay out of trouble, and don't take any more rides in trucks with pretty girls you don't know."

Thanksgiving was just a week away. Many families had lost loved ones and new plans had to be made for a Thanksgiving dinner. Who would host the gathering? Who would cook the meal? Who would bring what side dish? People who had never been close needed to come together. Some new relationships had developed, new wives or new husbands, new uncles and aunts. It would be the beginning of a new tradition.

Coming in off patrol, Lyle entered the office as Wayne was leaving. "Dad and I are having Thanksgiving dinner at Daryl and Patti's," he told Wayne, "Dad finally gets to meet the new in-laws to be."

Grinning, Wayne said, "I know Hiram will enjoy it. How's the work coming on the remodeling?"

"When the new stove gets here, the kitchen will be done. Bathroom is still getting the final touches."

"I'll be at Cassie's folks for the day," Wayne said. "Right now, I have to go to the butcher shop and pick out a chicken."

Laughing, Lyle said, "I'll save you a trip. Come out to the car."

Wayne admired the new Buick, asking "Does it have the Snuffy seal of approval?"

"It sure does," Lyle said, "and Edna loves it." Opening the rear door, Lyle reached in and handed Wayne a wrapped package.

"This is really heavy," Wayne said, "what is it?"

"Open it up," Lyle told him. Setting it on the hood, Wayne unwrapped it. His eyes got big and he stared at the biggest chicken he had ever seen. "It's a Rhode Island Red," Lyle said, "A gift to you and Billy from Daryl and Patti."

"I wonder how much it weighs," said Wayne.

"Just over 10 lbs.," Lyle answered proudly.

"I guess I'll be eating chicken for a week! Hey, Billy's in the office," Wayne said. "Let's go show him."

They took the package in, set it on Billy's desk and opened it. "It's as big as a turkey," Billy said. "I'll be eating chicken for a week!"

Calvin Jones had never felt more at peace. He had come to enjoy the farm lifestyle. Out of bed at 4:30 a.m. to do the morning milking. Feeding the cows, even cleaning the barn gave him a sense of purpose. He had learned to drive the tractor, harness and drive a team of horses and repair machinery. Regular meals had put some weight on him that had never been there before.

Virginia had given him what clothing of Jacob's that fit, even his boots were the right size. In the evening they talked. Dan and Ginnie wanted to know what it had been

like during the war. Ever so slowly, Calvin began to open up
and talk about his experience in uniform. This, he realized,
was where the peace came from. Telling someone he trusted
his thoughts and feelings about being a soldier. Sometimes
at night before bed, he knelt and prayed. 'I haven't done this
since I was a kid,' he thought, and it felt good.

CHAPTER THIRTY-FIVE

The first snowfall came the day after Thanksgiving. There had been a few light snows during early November, just a few inches, hardly enough to shovel. There was eight inches of fluffy white snow, and the men at the town garage were drawing straws to see who go to try out the new 1919 Chevrolet one-ton flatbed truck with a shiny new plow blade. Ernie Felker won the draw, and took Simon Luedke along as helper. All the men had practiced the hydraulic raising and lowering of the blade, now was the real test. The truck rolled out, the blade went down, and away Ernie went. It was 6 a.m., just light. At noon Ernie would return and someone else would take over.

The businesses along Main Street clapped and waved as Ernie went by. Another crew followed shoveling around the fire hydrants. Sidewalks were cleared by each business, town crews did the schools and court house. Schools were closed for the Thanksgiving weekend, and groups of boys roamed the town with shovels looking to earn some money. Churches had their own designated shovelers, as did the police force.

The energy was high, but by March people would be cursing the lovely gift from the heavens.

"I've got something for you men that you need to keep in the patrol car," Billy told Wayne and Lyle as they entered the office that morning. Billy pointed at two canvas bags sitting just inside the door. Opening them the deputy's each found a 25-foot length of chain with a hook on each end. "You'll either be pulling someone out of a ditch or someone will be pulling you out." then Billy laughed.

On County Road P, a logging truck was holding up traffic. A patch of ice under the snow had caused the rear tires of the trailer to slide into the ditch. With no traction, the truck didn't have the power to pull the trailer back up onto the road. Lyle drove to the nearest farm, that of Justin Reinholt. Justin agreed to take a look and see if his team could pull the trailer back on the road. He walked around the truck looking at the under carriage. "I'll need both teams, but I can do it," he said.

The driver shook his head and said "It's gonna take some mighty strong horses to move that trailer."

Grinning, Justin answered "then you're in luck, because that's what I have."

Lyle drove Justin back to the farm. Nancy came running from the house with a small wrapped package and handed it to Lyle. "I just took these cinnamon rolls out of the oven. Be careful they are still hot."

"You go on back to the truck, make sure the driver doesn't try to move it," Justin said, "Nancy and I will be along in about a half hour."

Very carefully, Justin hooked chains under the trailer. Nancy held both teams quiet while he worked, humming an old church hymn. 'It's like watching a child singing to a giant to make him go to sleep,' Lyle thought. Finally, Justin hooked the chains to the whiffletrees of the teams. "Take up the slack Nancy," he said quietly. With a cooing sound, Nancy led both teams ahead until the chains were taut.

Justin took the reins of the Belgians and Nancy the reins of the Suffolks. Together they started the teams forward. As the harnesses and chains pulled tight, the horses dug in. Slowly, the trailer began to move sideways. With a final shudder, the trailer was back on the road.

"WHOA!" Nancy and Justin yelled at the same time. Easing the teams back, Justin unhooked the chains.

"How much do I owe you," the driver asked. Justin looked at Nancy, who smiled and winked at him.

"My teams needed the exercise," Justin said with a grin, "No charge today. Be careful, there are a few other spots just like this one."

Waving, the driver started his truck and drove away. "Those were all pine logs," Justin said, "must be going to the paper mill."

"A lot of men who used to work in the brewery are now cutting pulp wood for the mills," Lyle said, "If you can swing an axe and handle a two-man saw, the mill will hire you."

With a wave, Lyle was back on patrol. He saw several farmers driving tractors with homemade wooden plows clearing their driveways. Back on the highway, the cars and trucks were moving slowly, following the snowplow. A Ford coupe was in the ditch so Lyle stopped.

Yelling down to the driver, Lyle asked "Is everyone alright?" An older man and his wife got out of the car. The man said, "Can we get a ride into town? My wife needs to catch the train."

Lyle helped them get up to his car with a suitcase. "I'll have the garage tow your car into town," Lyle said.

"Thank you so much," the woman said, "I'm heading to Wausau. Our granddaughter is having her first baby and I promised I would be there." Lyle dropped them at the train station then drove to Snuffy's garage.

"I'll get to it this afternoon," Snuffy told him. "It's been a busy morning."

It was late afternoon when Wayne got home. To his surprise, both the sidewalk and driveway were shoveled clean. He opened the door and stepped in.

"Take your boots off on the rug," Jan yelled from the kitchen.

"Did you do all the shoveling?" Wayne asked.

Jan said, "No. Two big strong boys with shovels came looking for work. For fifty cents apiece, they did a good job." Wayne handed her a dollar bill, which she stuffed in her pocket. "I was pretty sure you would be hungry after a hard, cold day, so I made chicken soup with buttermilk biscuits."

"Sit down and eat with me," Wayne said, "and I'll tell you about my fun day."

CHAPTER THIRTY-SIX

The Marshfield News headline read: GOVERNOR DECLARES FLU IS OVER! Wisconsin Governor Emanuel Philipp held a news conference in Madison stating there had not been a single case of the flu reported in Wisconsin for two months, the last being a young woman who had recovered and was back home. The death toll would not be available until February of 1920 when all the research was completed.

"Some guy in Chicago is working on a siren that can be mounted on a patrol car," Billy told his deputies. "It will be run off the battery and is operated by the driver with a switch mounted on the dashboard."

"When will it be ready?" Wayne asked.

"The guy says the Chicago police will test it next month," Billy answered.

"I sure hope it works," Lyle said, "just honking the horn doesn't always make drivers stop."

Wayne and Cassie were enjoying an evening out. They started with a trip to the theater. A new film—'Almost a

Husband' starring Will Rogers and Peggy Wood. On the way out of the theater, Wayne said, "Did you know Will Rogers started as a cowboy in Oklahoma, then joined Buffalo Bill's Wild West Show before becoming an actor?"

"Yes, I did," Cassie said, "But I enjoy you telling me about it."

Laughing together, they walked to the Marshfield Hotel for dinner.

"You haven't told me what you would like for Christmas," Wayne said. "Have you thought about it?"

Squeezing Wayne's arm, Cassie said, "I have thought about it, and I would like a book."

"That's it?" Wayne asked.

"That's it" Cassie answered. "A journalist, John Reed, has been covering the Russian revolution, and has written a book titled 'Ten Days That Shook the World.' It tells how the revolution started, and where it is now."

Nodding his head, Wayne said, "You shall have it, and when you've finished reading it, tell me your thoughts."

"I promise," Cassie said. "And what is your wish for Christmas?"

"A new hat," Wayne said. "Since I got home, I've been wearing my father's hat. I would like one of my own."

At the hotel dining room, they ordered steaks, baked potato and coffee. "This will be my last Christmas as just a daughter," Cassie sighed, "It's exciting, but also sad."

"Why sad?" Wayne asked.

"It means we're entering a new phase of our life," Cassie said, "and leaving our families to become a new family. Mom and Dad will be alone, and that is sad."

176

"In that case, we must give them grandchildren as quickly as possible," said Wayne.

Cassie began giggling and couldn't stop. Finally, she said "Mom and I talked today about that very thing, and she agrees with you!"

Jan was having lunch with her sister Millie at Carson's Cafe. "I can't thank you enough for getting me the job at Wayne Schooley's house," Jan said. "That young man is the finest person I have ever worked for. He treats me like family."

Patting her hand, Millie said, "What will you do after Wayne and Cassie are married?"

Grinning, Jan said, "I will still be working there. They both want me to stay on because both of them will be working long hours."

"They do make a lovely couple and that other deputy, Lyle Peterson, is marrying Daryl and Patti Weber's daughter, Edna."

Laughing, Jan said, "I really like Edna, she reminds me of me!"

Wayne and Lyle were going out to Claude Bettendorf's farm to cut two Christmas trees, one for each family. Claude had called Billy with the offer, and Billy accepted.

"He's still happy Gandt's still blowing up," Bill said laughing.

Years ago, Claude had planted some pines just for Christmas trees. He kept them pruned and trimmed. Picking out two nice six footers, Wayne took them both down with the axe. They dragged them back to the car, tied them down, thanked Claude, and drove home.

In the evening, as the sun was setting, Main Street Marshfield looked like a Christmas village. Each shop had window decorations with lights and wreaths around the doors. The street lights were hung with wreaths decorated with red and green bows.

A week before Christmas the churches gathered their flocks and went caroling through their respective neighborhoods. Two local farmers offered sleigh rides in the park. The manger scene was the pride and joy of the volunteer firemen. They had sent all the way to St. Louis, Missouri for the glazed plaster statues and had built the stable themselves.

The week leading up to Christmas day, when Main Street traffic was at its busiest, many warnings were given out, but not one ticket. Santa Clause made several surprise visits to St. Joseph's hospital carrying a bag of small gifts for the patients who would not be at home. Each school had its own small pageant, and the high school chorus had been practicing for weeks for their event at the high school auditorium on Christmas eve.

"What time would you like me to be here tomorrow morning?" Wayne asked Cassie. They had been to the high school chorus with Billy and Helen, now they were saying good night.

"I'll be up early," Cassie said. "If you are here at 6 o'clock, I'll have coffee ready and we can talk and cuddle before Mom and Dad wake up."

"I already put your present under the tree, but no peeking until tomorrow," Wayne said.

As they hugged, Cassie said softly, "Next year, we will have our own home, our own tree and our own Christmas."

"What a year this has been," Wayne said. "It started in France and will end in your living room."

"Let's hope 1920 will treat us well" Cassie said, "because I plan to be a very happy Mrs. Wayne Schooley."

The End

ABOUT THE AUTHOR

Mark Gengler was born and raised on a small farm north of Medford, Wisconsin. He joined the U.S. Army in 1963 and was stationed at Fort Bragg, N.C., with the 82nd Airborne Division. He saw action in the Dominican Republic in 1965. After his discharge, he traveled America, working odd jobs in California, Texas, Colorado, Kansas City and New Orleans. He returned to Wisconsin and went to broadcasting school on the G.I. Bill. Mr. Gengler was a disc-jockey, got married, and went to work at the University of Wisconsin, Oshkosh, until retiring in 2003.

*Other Titles
by Mark Gengler*

NOAH THORNE
A WISCONSIN FARM BOY IN THE 1920'S

THANKS A LOT GOD

WOLF CREEK CIDER
THE STORY OF AARON STROUD

MIGRANT!
THE STORY OF DANNY BROOME

MARSHFIELD 1919
THE STORY OF WAYNE SCHOOLEY

Published by
Christopher Matthews Publishing
an imprint of First Steps Publishing
FirstStepsPublishing.com